Items should be returned  shown below. Items not al borrowers may be renewe telephone. To renew, plea barcode label. To renew This can be requested at your local library. Renew online @ **www.dublincitypubliclibraries.ie** Fines charged for overdue items will include postage incurred in recovery. Damage to or loss of items will be charged to the borrower.

Leabharlanna Poiblí Chathair Bhaile Átha Cliath
Dublin City Public Libraries

Alex Miller is an overall winner of the Commonwealth Writers' Prize for *The Ancestor Game*. Published internationally and widely in translation, his novels have received critical acclaim in all territories. His eleven novels have been shortlisted in all the major literary awards and have won many of them.

In 2008, *Landscape of Farewell* won the Chinese Annual Foreign Novels 21st Century Award and the Manning Clark Medal for an outstanding contribution to Australian cultural life.

In 2012, Alex Miller was awarded the Melbourne Prize for Literature for his body of work.

In 2014, *Coal Creek* was awarded the Victorian Premier's Prize for Literature.

'*Coal Creek* is at once a heart-rending novel one feels compelled to read in one or two sittings, and a thought-provoking narrative that raises profound ethical questions about loyalty, redemption and forgiveness... This is an Australian evocation of some of the same preoccupations and convictions American writers such as Faulkner and Steinbeck tried to express. Miller is that rare writer at once able to register how nuances of class and regional difference inflect people's life choices, while also having confidence in the capacity of the human soul to circumvent these worldly definitions. Though the latest of a series of impressive novels Miller has produced, *Coal Creek* is definitely the best place for a newcomer to Miller's vision to begin.'

—From the Victorian Premier's Prize for Fiction citation

www.alexmiller.com.au

Praise for *Coal Creek*

'Alex Miller's *Coal Creek* is a triumph. If ever there were an example of a novelist simultaneously commanding yet somehow at the mercy of a character's voice, this is it.'
— Tim Winton, *The Australian*, Best Books of 2013

'Miller has been a master of visceral description from as long ago as the first novel he published...What might also be considered are the likenesses, more than ever apparent, between his career and that of Patrick White. Each draws deeply on his youthful experience working in the outback. Each writes of the making of art. They are alike adept at acrid comedies of manners.'
— *Weekend Australian*

'It's difficult to shake off the sense that in *Coal Creek* Miller has struck a kind of grace note in a literary career already lauded for a certain touch of resonant genius. For *Coal Creek* is that rare, mystifyingly powerful novel that lodges itself, unbidden, deep in the human marrow... Miller brings a rare empathy and melodic power to this tale which is, at one level, a timeless tale of friendship and love, betrayal and injustice. At another it is like a ballad to country – timeless, evocative, and unforgettable.'
— *West Australian*

'Miller's voice is never more pure or lovely than when he channels it through an instrument as artless as Bobby Blue... The intelligence of the author haunts the novel, like an atmosphere.'
— *The Monthly*

'A heartbreaking tale of love and friendship.'
— *Adelaide Advertiser*

'Bold, but brilliant, his simple voice turn[s] this tangled tale of love, friendship and misunderstanding into something both powerful and deeply moving.'
— *Australian Women's Weekly*

'Miller's 11th novel deserves a place in the national psyche alongside *Picnic at Hanging Rock*.'
— *Herald Sun*, Best Books of 2013

Praise for *Autumn Laing*

'. . . in many respects Miller's best yet . . . a penetrating and moving examination of long-dead dreams and the ravages of growing old.'
— *Times Literary Supplement*

'A beautiful book.'
— *Irish Times*

'Such riches. All of Alex Miller's wisdom and experience—of art, of women and what drives them, of writing, of men and their ambitions—and every mirage and undulation of the Australian landscape are here, transmuted into rare and radiant fiction. An indispensable novel.'
— *Australian Book Review*

'That Alex Miller in a seemingly effortless fashion is able to gouge out the innermost recesses of the artistic soul in his latest novel, *Autumn Laing*, speaks volumes about the command he has of his craft and the insights that a lifetime of wrestling with his own creative impulses has brought. Miller has invested this story of art and passion with his own touch of genius and it is, without question, a triumph of a novel.'
— *Canberra Times, Panorama*

'Miller has fun with his cast of characters and humour, while black, ripples through the narrative, leavening Autumn's more corrosive judgements and insights. Miller engages so fully with his female characters that divisions between the sexes seem to melt away and all stand culpable, vulnerable, human on equal ground. Miller is also adept at taking abstract concepts—about art or society—and securing them in the convincing form of his complex, unpredictable characters and their vivid interior monologues.'
— *The Monthly*

'Few writers have Miller's ability to create tension of this depth out of old timbers such as guilt, jealousy, selfishness, betrayal, passion and vision. *Autumn Laing* is more than just beautifully crafted. It is inhabited by characters whose reality challenges our own.'
— *Saturday Age, Life & Style*

Praise for *Lovesong*

'With *Lovesong*, one of our finest novelists has written perhaps his finest book . . . *Lovesong* explores, with compassionate attentiveness, the essential solitariness of people. Miller's prose is plain, lucid, yet full of plangent resonance.'
— *The Age*

'Miller's brilliant, moving novel captures exactly that sense of a storybuilt life—wonderful and terrifying in equal measure, stirring and abysmal, a world in which both heaven and earth remain present, yet stubbornly out of reach.'
— *Sunday Age*

'*Lovesong* is a limpid and elegant study of the psychology of love and intimacy. The characterisation is captivating and the framing metafictional narrative skilfully constructed.'
— *Australian Book Review*

'. . . a ravishing, psychologically compelling work from one of our best . . .'
— *Courier Mail*

'. . . another triumph: lyrical, soothing and compelling. Miller enriches human fragility with literary beauty . . .'
— *Newcastle Herald*

'The intertwining stories are told with gentleness, some humour, some tragedy and much sweetness. Miller is that rare writer who engages the intellect and the emotions simultaneously, with a creeping effect.'
— *Bookseller & Publisher*

'With exceptional skill, Miller records the ebb and flow of emotion . . . *Lovesong* is a poignant tale of infidelity; but it is more than that. It is a manifesto for the novel, a tribute to the human rite of fiction with the novelist officiating.'
— *Australian Literary Review*

ALEX MILLER

Coal Creek

ALLEN&UNWIN

First published in Great Britain in 2014 by Allen & Unwin
This paperback edition published in 2015

Allen & Unwin
c/o Atlantic Books
Ormond House
26–27 Boswell Street
London WC1N 3JZ
Phone: 020 7269 1610
Fax: 020 7430 0916
Email: UK@allenandunwin.com
Web: www.allenandunwin.co.uk

A CIP catalogue record for this book is available from the British Library.

Paperback ISBN 978 1 74331 945 1
Ebook ISBN 978 1 74343 557 1

Text design by Lisa White
Set in Minion Pro by Bookhouse, Sydney
Printed in Italy by Grafica Veneta S.p.A.

10 9 8 7 6 5 4 3 2 1

For Stephanie

And for Ross, Kate & Erin

PART ONE

ONE

My mother told me and Charley when we was children, Saint Paul said God has chosen the weak things of the world, the foolish things of the world, the base things of the world and those things which are despised. We all hang on the cross, she said. Whenever she seen I was suffering she touched my cheek and smiled her sad smile and said it to me: We all hang on the cross, Bobby Blue. Don't you forget it. And that is what she always called me, her Bobby Blue. I was the youngest and her favourite of the two of us. Even as a boy Charley was always making off somewhere on his own. He had red hair and the rest of us was all dark-haired. I don't think he ever felt like he was really one of us. I do still regret even at this time of my life not being with my mother when she closed her eyes for the last time and said her goodbyes to us and to this world, as I know she would have done even though we was not with her to hear her words of love and farewell. They have always burned in my mind, those words I never heard. I hear them now. She died without having no illness first, so there was no warning given me and Dad. By that time I thought I was a man, though I was still only a boy. I was out in the camp mustering the scrubs with Dad, and our Charley had gone off to the coast to get away from Dad's impatience with him.

Me and Dad learned Mother had died when we rode into town and was yarding the bullocks for Mr Dawson at the railhead. It was George Wilson, the constable at Mount Hay in them days, who come out to the holding yards in that Dodge pick-up truck he had then and told Dad that Mum was dead a week. Old George Wilson with his sagging moustache and his sagging khaki police uniform, which made him look sad, his big Webley revolver holstered on his right hip with the flap of the holster buckled down, which always had me thinking he would not want to get taken by surprise. And that never happened anyhow, except in my imagination, where I seen him shot in the chest and going to his knees, his fingers still fussing with the buckle of that holster. But the truth is I never seen George unholster that weapon and I doubt very much he ever did, but he always wore it. Just in case, I suppose. He stood alongside the chute that day, his sweated-up old police slouch hat in one hand, looking solemn and touching his moustache with the fingers of his other hand. I had noticed before how George was always nervous around my dad and stood back from him, like he feared my dad might blame him for bad news. Giving Dad a bit of room, which was George Wilson's way with trouble of any kind. Not that my dad was a man for trouble, but he was a silent man and he did not smile a lot, and that made people careful around him.

It was at that time of the late afternoon when the wind used to get up and them long grey clouds come floating in from the desert out west, as if they had once rained somewhere, casting sudden shadows across the stockyards and making the cattle restless. The beasts was setting up one great racket of bellowing and it was hard to hear what George was saying but I knew it was something important. I do not remember Dad answering nothing to George at the time but just pausing to listen, in the way my dad had, respecting the man, until George had finished telling his news, then getting on with dipping the beasts for ticks that we was in the middle of doing.

Dad never did have much to say unless he was angry with you, then you heard from him. If Dad wanted me to do something when we was out mustering he raised his whip hand and indicated. He knew I would be keeping an eye on him, like a man playing in a brass band has one eye on the bandmaster and the other eye on the music. That is the way all them old fellows did it. They indicated. And we understood them. They never had a lot of time for yelling and carrying on like people do today. Rip-tear-and-bust was not their style. Working in the scrubs alongside them there was just the trample of the beasts making their way through the timber ahead of your horse and them cows and calves that was separated bellowing to find each other. It was such a familiar music I believe we stopped hearing it. It was just there in our daily life. They was good days we had together and I will not forget them. If my dad seen the bad way my life and Ben's went after he was gone over to the other side he would wish he might have had the chance to step in and redirect us with one of those indicating signs of his long before we was too far caught up in that trouble. Dad would have seen the trouble coming to us, the way he seen trouble coming when we was out in the scrubs. He had an ear for it. I seen him raise his head and listen many times when we was at supper around our fire out in the camps, and I would know something was up. But he would not speak of it till it was time to speak of it.

. . .

I did not weep out at the yards that day I heard my mother had been dead a week but I wept when I was on my own later. And since that day I have wept for my mother many times, thinking of her love for us all and her special regard for me that I was never to know again from any woman but one. Me and Dad buried my mother up there in the cemetery behind the town reservoir and everyone in town come to her funeral and walked up the hill behind me and Dad and Ben Tobin and his dad who were all carrying her coffin. Which weighed very little. At the graveside I seen my dad was weeping, his hat held in his hands in front of him, his face uncovered to the crowd and his grief at the loss of his beloved companion plain for everyone to see and no shame in him. It was the only time I ever seen my dad weep and it moved me greatly and my grief caught me in my chest and I wept with him. Charley did not get back from the coast for it.

It was ten or eleven years later when I buried Dad up there beside Mum and alongside Ben's dad, who died of lung cancer. Dad had an accident off his horse and took a while to go. I was home with him holding his hand the evening he went. He was in pain and I believe he was not sorry to leave it behind. The last words he said to me was, I love you, son. It was good to hear that from him and I have cherished them words ever since, hearing him say them often in my mind when I have struck a patch of trouble. My dad believed in me and in my ability out there in the scrubs and nothing made me prouder than to have that belief and trust from him, and to know it in myself. He was the finest horseman I ever knew. I seen him step into a yard with a wild horse and him and that horse working partners together by the end of that same day, and nothing said about it. That is just how it was with him and horses. No one never made nothing of it. He never raised his voice to an animal, nor his whip. He had it from my grandfather, who raised him in the bendee and the brigalow scrubs in the steady way they had in them days. Hard men they were, but with a belief and a grace in them and in their actions that we do not see in men now. It has been forgotten. I do not know why. I had no way of contacting Charley for our dad's funeral but I said a prayer for him beside the grave so my older brother would not be left out of it. There was a loneliness in me for my mother, knowing Charley was not there. I cannot explain it. That was the way of our family and there is no more to be said of it.

My mother died alone without her sons or her husband at her side, but I do not think the people of Mount Hay thought that circumstance unusual in them days. There was no town further west after Mount Hay, just them two big cattle runs, the Stanbys' Assumption Downs, and they was English people, and that family out at Preference whose name I never could remember, it was Irish. But no actual town till you crossed the border into the Territory. But I never went that far west and I never heard of no town over the border except what they used to call the Wheel. I am not sure if the Wheel is in the Territory or is still in the state of Queensland. Like I said, I never been out there and I have no picture of the Wheel in my head but only the name. Mount Hay was the end of the line then and still is as far as I know that country.

I never missed visiting my mother's grave on the anniversary of her death except if we was out in the camps. But I never seen Dad go up there to the cemetery. I think he did not wish to be reminded his wife was dead. It was a sad fact that had come into his life and he could forget it when we was out in the camps. My mother never had been out in the camps with him and it was normal to be without her. He only seen her when we come back into town. It was 1946 or 47 when Dad died. I know the facts but I am not reliable around dates and numbers, so do not hold me to the year exactly. Things changed for me at that time. By then I was twenty years of age, I suppose, and Daniel Collins come out of the army, and that is when this trouble that I am giving an account of here started. With Dad gone and Ben's dad already dead the old days was over for us and I needed to look around and find a new way for myself to make a living. The stations would have been happy to put me on and I might have stuck with the cattle work but the job with the new constable come up just then and I thought I would give it a go just for a short time. I did not expect things to work out the way they did.

. . .

Daniel Collins had served as a volunteer with the Australian forces in New Guinea during the war and after he come out he joined the Queensland Police Service. When we got Daniel as the new constable at Mount Hay his older girl, Irie, was twelve years of age, or around that, and the younger was maybe nine or ten. I was not sure at the time of their ages. Esme and Daniel soon got close again after the war, which was not how it worked out for every man who come back. Esme was a determined woman and was firm in her high principles. The police in Brisbane, where Daniel done his induction, told him he could apply for the bush but he had to be a horseman. He told them he knew something about horses, but I do not think Daniel Collins ever knew too much about horses. He applied for the constable job out at Mount Hay which come vacant when old George Wilson finally give it away. George was the constable at Mount Hay for around thirty years, and if trouble ever happened in George's time he always give it a bit of clearance to sort itself out before stepping in. Which usually turned out he had no cause to step in too hard in any case as things had more or less worked themselves out by the time he roused himself.

George believed in something he called a natural peace. Which some people said was bone laziness by another name. But to my way of thinking there was a wisdom in George Wilson's method of policing our town. The gold mining was pretty well played out by that time and there was only a handful of the old hopefuls left fossicking the known seams and mullock heaps, and the stockmen from them big stations seldom come into town more than once or twice in a year and kicked up a bit of a party. George only ever had two murders in his whole time as the Mount Hay constable and there was never a robbery I ever heard of. Cattle duffing was a usual pastime with some of the young fellers on the stations but it never got too serious and everyone knew who was doing it and it was soon put a stop to. Mount Hay was not a troubled town like they say the Isa was. Though I have never been to the Isa and that is only hearsay from me and cannot be trusted for the facts.

Dad dying and George Wilson retiring and the war ending all happened around the same time and the way I had been living out in the camps most of the year come to an end. I did not think too much about applying for the constable's offsider job but just went over and asked Daniel about giving the job to me and we shook hands and he agreed to take me on. George Wilson never had no offsider but Daniel Collins announced at the pub that he was entitled to put one on. We all seen Daniel's intention was to do the job by the book. Which was the first notice we had of the changes. If I had known what was going to happen between Ben and Daniel I would have thought more about it and kept out of the way. But I just seen it as a job at the time, which I was in need of.

The police in Brisbane laughed at Daniel and told him to be careful not to die of boredom out there in the ranges, which they called the wilderness. But Daniel was interested in all kinds of things and not just in policing so he said he would risk getting bored. He believed he had missed out on some of his best years fighting in the war and wanted to make up for lost time. At least that is what he told me. It was an adventure for him and his family to go out there to Mount Hay and I do not think they was ever intending to spend more than a couple of years in the ranges at the outside, but seen it as something they could look back on and talk about when they was back in the city again. Daniel and Esme seen it as a challenge to improve things in Mount Hay. But they would have done better to hold off a while like George Wilson, till they got a feel for the way things was done. But that was not their way.

To people like the Collins, Mount Hay was what they called the outback, but to us it was just Mount Hay. If they ever heard of it people in Mount Hay did not know where the outback was, but Daniel and Esme seemed to be sure of knowing they was already in it, which was the cause of a good deal of amusement in the bar of Chiller Swales' hotel. The way I saw it was that Daniel and Esme never thought too much about how it was going to be for them coming in to police a town like Mount Hay from outside the way they did. They surely thought we was a bunch of country hicks and they knew better than we did how to do things and did not think they had nothing to learn. But they had never been out in country like the ranges before and was coastal people. In the ranges everyone knows everyone else for hundreds of miles around. And we always knew if there was a stranger around and would have him pinpointed exactly. Strangers was rare. Old George had grown up in the ranges and knew the way things was done. Daniel knew other things. He had books on the geology of the inland and the local people and history and he was proposing to do some reading of those books he brought with him and become an expert on us.

. . .

Mount Hay main street was just the police office and house at the back, and beside it on both sides there was empty blocks of land with only the stumps of old houses left on them. Down the road towards the west and on the opposite side from the police office was Hoy's milk bar and grocery store, which was also the postal office. There was a couple of unoccupied shops, both with their front windows broken in and sheets of ripple iron nailed over them, and then come Chiller Swales' hotel. The picture theatre down the road by the corner before you head out west had been burned down some years before and never got rebuilt. There was the tennis courts, which had not been used since I was a child and was all overgrown with rattlepod, and then the public hall that was sliding off its stumps, its timbers pretty much eaten out by white ants. The only fuel pump in town was at the side of Hoy's place. That was about it. Except for the school, a hundred yards further along than the burned picture theatre. I do not know why they put the school so far away, but maybe they thought the town would grow out to meet it. But it never did. The kids from the outlying stations come in as well as the town kids. They was like two tribes and was always fighting. It was black kids and white kids at the school in them days but that changed later when the government brought in new ideas. People was generally scattered about the township in timber and fibro cement houses. Like Mum and Dad's old place. When someone died or left town their place usually stayed empty. There was a few of them abandoned houses around. I rode past our old place one day and seen some town boys had kicked in the fibro panels and shot out most of the windows. Which was usually what happened when a house was left empty. I thought of burning it, but I did not do that and rode on. I suppose it is still there to this day, what is left of the old place.

There was no real centre to Mount Hay like there had once been. Goats come along the street and eat everything. The dogs got sick of chasing them off and just lay in the shade with their head on their paws and give a tired kind of woof if the goats got too close to them. The mail delivery truck went to the coast twice a week and brought in stores and drums of fuel for the town and the outlying people. If you was willing to leave people alone to get on with whatever they was doing, which was what George Wilson always done, then I would say Mount Hay was not a hard town to police.

After Dad passed away and I started as Daniel's offsider, Esme made me welcome and had me eating with her and Daniel and the girls in the kitchen of the police house. I did not camp in the house with them, but in the fibro two-man quarters at the back of the police block. Which suited me as it was next to the horse paddock and the feed shed, where I spent a good deal of my time. After I started I did not wait to be told by Daniel nothing of what needed to be done but put shoes on the police horses and took care of them without saying nothing to him. Which was the way we always worked when Dad and Ben's dad were alive. If we seen something needed doing we done it and no one said nothing about it. There was two horses belonging to the police and my two, so I was not kept real busy. Dad's old packhorse, Beau, was the boss of all the horses as soon as I put him in the paddock. He nearly had them two police horses through the fence in their panic. Beau and my mare Mother was close as brother and sister and them police horses could not get near Mother without Beau driving them. It took them all a week or two to sort themselves out and know where they stood with each other. They never become close friends but they learned to live with each other without going through the fences.

By then I had forgot the little of reading and writing I'd picked up in that school we had in Mount Hay in them days, and being out in the camps with Dad since I was ten my mother never did get the chance to teach me nothing, even though she would have liked to. It was Daniel and Esme's older girl, Irie, that taught me to read and write properly, or I would not be writing this account of the trouble that come on us now. The young one, Miriam, mocked me for not knowing my schoolwork but Irie never did, she just set to and helped me learn. Irie had brown hair and very pale skin like her dad. If she went out in the sun without her hat she burned to red in no time. She was gentle and respectful when instructing me but there was a steel spring in that girl that would unwind in a flash like a whip when she was pushed. She did not accept advice or criticism from her mother Esme or from Daniel without backing up against them. And she kept to her own thoughts. I seen that at once and admired her for it. I was very soon more than half in love with her though she was yet but a child. I liked the independent way she carried herself and I seen she was soon going to be the kind of woman my mother and father would have had a high opinion of. I wish they had known her. If Charley had been more like her when I was a kid I would have had an older brother as a friend to look out for me and maybe I would not have got so close to Ben as I did. But Charley was always a loner. I never knew what his thoughts was or where he went when he headed off on his own. And I never wanted to be like him. Him and Dad never hit it off and Dad was always rounding on him for something. Charley was not interested in stock work and had no admiration for our dad and his ways. He looked upon our father with some fear and could not be open with him about his thoughts. Dad could not stand that. My mother used to say our Charley was born different, and she would shake her head and say there was no use trying to make him change. Charley is himself, she said and she told Dad he should be content with that. But Dad could not be content in this way about his older son and always remained disappointed in Charley, carrying an anger against him. He was harder on Charley than he ever was on me and I seen how Charley resented that and could not wait for the day when he was grown enough to leave Mount Hay and get out on his own. Which is what he did.

I never heard Dad speak of him after that, but my mother used to look up from what she was doing some evenings and say to no one in particular, I wonder where our Charley is now? We did not hear from him. I have wondered if he resented me for being my mother's favourite. And that has given me feelings of regret that I did not try to help him when the chance was there. I will not look to excuse myself now.

Daniel encouraged me to read them books he had on geology and history but I was not a good enough reader in them days to make sense of them. At first he was always wanting to talk with me about things in Mount Hay and what I thought of this or that family. He come down to the yards where I was tending to the horses and asked me about the old days and my father and all that, but I was never much of a talker. I pretended to him that what he said was interesting to me because I could see he wanted me to enjoy his company, but I never knew what he was talking about most of the time. My dad would have took one look at Daniel Collins and he would have walked away and not looked back. Thinking of the way Dad would have seen him I sometimes had the flicker of what you might call contempt in myself for Daniel, but it was something I rebuked myself for as I only knew him to be a good man and never deserving of anyone's harsh judgment. Because he and Esme was from the coast did not make them bad people, just different. I remember a photo in one of them books of his. It was of a man standing next to an anthill holding a long stick upright in his hand. I do not know if the photo was to show how tall the anthill was or how tall the man was or how long the stick was, or maybe all three. But I remember looking at that picture for some time and wondering about it. And I still have a good memory of it today. The man was without a hat, which was unusual then and may be why I remember that picture. I do not know who the man was. It did not say and I did not ask. Who he was did not seem like something I would ever need to know.

We never asked too many questions about things we did not want to know about. And even with things we wanted to know about we waited to find out and kept our questions to ourselves and mostly they got answered by events. But Daniel was not like us in that and was always asking questions. He stood out from the people of the ranges and you seen he would never be one of us. If me and him was meeting with Chiller at the pub or with Allan Hoy or his missus at the store, Daniel would be asking them about this and that, how old was their kids and how long had they been there and where did they live before they come to Mount Hay. And I seen how uneasy his questions was making everyone. There were times I found it hard to listen to him. But that was his habit of open curiosity, and it come to stand between him and a good many of the people in Mount Hay, me included, though I would say I liked him well enough in a general way. Others come straight out and said he was a damn fool and would not last long and they made sure to avoid him if they seen him coming. If I did not know the true answers to his questions, I made up answers out of my head to please him and he never seemed to mind me doing that and I do not know if he ever noticed I was doing it, though I think Esme did as she give me a bit of a look if I come up with some answer she thought was just too fancy. Daniel wrote my answers in the notebook he always kept in the breast pocket of his police shirt, as if he thought writing down my answers was making them more true than they was. I have very little memory of the things I told him. I would say whatever come to me at the moment. Harmless lies mostly, I suppose. It pleased me to see him listening to whatever I said, nodding his head and fingering his pencil, ready to place my words in his record, just like he thought I was the expert on Mount Hay.

Esme and me had some understanding of this that we did not share with Daniel and we did not even share it openly with each other, but it was just there between us by signs. Because a thing is not in the open does not mean it is not there. I was young and so was she. I respected her and at first I liked her, but I feared too what she might bring about with her high principles and I was not mistaken in that fear, as we shall see. But you cannot tell another person how to change their ways and I did not try to tell Daniel's wife how she might change herself to suit Mount Hay instead of trying to change Mount Hay to suit herself. Which I knew she would never succeed in. The people of Mount Hay was who they was and that was that. People of the ranges. And they mostly despised the people of the coast and laughed at them and their peculiar way of going on.

. . .

That first year went by and everything was quiet in Mount Hay, like the coppers at the headquarters on the coast had predicted it would be for Daniel and Esme and their two girls. An adventure holiday in the wild scrubs of the ranges for this city family. Daniel made himself busy in the office trying to put George Wilson's piles of old records into some kind of order. I never seen Daniel without a fresh shave and a clean ironed shirt. He liked to see things sitting square and straight. I think he seen George's records as the main challenge for him. Most people was friendly to them on the surface and Esme got the tennis club going again and Irie was a good tennis player and there was always some working bee or other Esme was trying to get people together for. But I think she soon began to see how people's interest in what she was doing did not last long. Ballroom dancing was something she had going for a while. Then it drifted off and come to an end, like most other things she did. The Mount Hay women lost interest in her way of pushing and prodding them and they soon began to resent her and to laugh at her behind her back. I guess she dismissed their ways as of no account and that is what they resented. But many of them had the habit of laziness and did not want to change.

Esme must have begun to feel a bit shut out by the other women and as time went on she turned her attention more to the police house and to her own family and began to leave the people of the town to get on as best they could without her help. Which they had been doing well enough before she come into the town. Esme got a vegetable and flower garden going at the police house for a while but the weather did not suit vegetables and the goats kept getting in when people left the gate open. Struggling with that took up a lot of her spare time for a while. In the first months Daniel went out exploring into the scrubs a few times. That is what he called it, exploring, like no one had been out there ahead of him. He set off on foot but I do not think he went more than a few hundred yards off from the house. He started out collecting plants and looking for rock paintings and sacred stone arrangements and that kind of thing. But his enthusiasm for it petered out and he began to spend most of his time in the office trying to get them records of George's into a perfect order. He was impressed knowing I had spent pretty much my entire life out in the camps with my dad and his partner, Ben Tobin's dad. He was always asking me which of the local Aborigines he should talk to for information about their beliefs and their way of life. I pointed him at this or that individual who I knew was going to tell him they did not know where the sacred places he was talking about was at. Which is their way. To deny knowing stuff when they don't want you to know it. It is what most people do in my experience, black and white. It's what we kids did at school when the teachers asked us something. I don't know. You heard it every day. The Aborigines I sent him to put Daniel off the scent by telling him to go and see someone who they was having a feud with, just to get a laugh to see him bothering their enemy with his fool questions. They was so polite to him it was a wonder he did not see they was fooling around with him.

I heard Daniel telling Esme one time that the Aborigines knew nothing about their own country and they all hated each other. There was always some fight going on between this or that family. Which was only natural. Daniel was putting together a collection of stone tools and I or anyone else could have told him where to find plenty of them things but I seen he liked to think he was finding stuff no one else knew about, so I left him to it. He was interested in things we did not care about and he liked to talk about his plans to everyone. But they did not wish to hear his plans.

I followed Daniel one day on Mother. I had that mare from when she was a foal and I always called her Mother, which was to honour the memory of my own mother. Watching Daniel walking around in the scrub looking for stuff that day I soon seen he never knew he was being watched. I knew from that he was not the man for that country. A man for that country knows when he is being watched and he will make some sign to let you know he is on to you and he does not care if you are watching him or not and will go about his own business, and if you wish to speak with him then you will come up to him and say whatever you wish to say, but if you are just passing along then that is what you will do and you will not disturb him. But he will still make a sign to let you know he knows you are there. The old fellers, black and white, never talked or made no noise when they was riding through the scrubs and you seldom seen them get their horse out of a walk unless they was dogging a micky or heading a bunch of wild cows, but they seen everything and would come back over their tracks at the end of the day and pick up beasts or get honey from a nest they had seen in the morning when they was going out. They never said nothing about seeing beasts camped under the limes or seeing honey in a hollow crotch of a lancewood tree. They seen

24

it. And if you had not seen it that was too bad for you. They was not going to tell you about it. The man who did not see such things was counted a fool, and what point was there in telling a fool something?

If you was with Daniel in the scrub and he seen something he was quick to point it out to you, like he thought you had not seen it and he wanted to let you know he had seen it first. Like he was scoring a point over you. That day I followed him I watched him looking around but seeing nothing. He crossed my tracks that day without seeing them. I never told him I had been watching him and he did not know.

. . .

It was mid-morning and I was out by the side fence to the garden fixing the hang of the gate when Esme called me in for a cup of tea, which was our usual time for smoko. Daniel had gone down the coast for some meeting or other with his senior people in Townsville and the girls was at school. Sitting across from Esme at the table in the kitchen drinking my tea and eating the Anzac biscuits she had cooked that morning, I seen the way Esme was looking at me, her eyes on me in a steady way that made me feel I had better say something. I said, These biscuits are as good as my mother's biscuits was. When I said this Esme gave me a big smile and she said back at me, You are very welcome, Bobby. We sat on again in silence a while and I was hurrying my tea to get back out to my work on the gate when she said, I would like you to read to me from the book Irie is teaching you with. Will you do that for me? I said I would do it gladly but I did not think I was that good a reader yet. Esme got up and she fetched the book from the dresser where it was kept with the other books and she set it in front of me and sat beside me so she could look over my shoulder. I did not feel at my ease with her sitting so close to me. She was a fine-looking woman and I had often admired her from a distance, but I would have been upset if she had ever guessed my admiration. I opened the book and cleared my throat and I began to read from the early part of the book, which I knew by then pretty well. As I read I could hear Irie's voice reading them same words and it gave me confidence and I soon began to relax. When I turned over the page to go on, Esme put her hand on my hand to stop me and she said, Thank you, Bobby. I looked at her and seen she was moved by her thoughts. She took her hand off mine and closed the book and she said, I am very proud of you. I hope you know how welcome you are here among my family. I could think of nothing to say to this, so I said nothing, but looked down at the book and hoped we was done.

From time to time after that, when I was about the place doing some chore or other, and the girls was at school and Daniel was in the office doing his records or making calls to the police in Townsville, Esme asked me to read to her and I did so. I would not say this become a habit with us, but it was something I began to enjoy, and I believe she did too. Being on our own like that in the kitchen with me reading and her listening the way she always did, as if it all meant something to her, it was like we had become friends. When I thought about it later on, I seen that after all her plans for improving Mount Hay come to nothing, Esme must have begun to see me as her one and only Mount Hay success. I had been learning from the beginning to please Irie, who I felt myself to be very close to, but soon I was also learning to please Esme, so she would not feel her belief in me was mistaken. We got used to each other's company at those times. I told her stories of my childhood and my mother and she always listened as if she was hearing something of great interest to her. She never told me nothing about her own childhood. So I can tell nothing of it here.

One of them times when I had been reading to her and was about to go on out to get on with my work, Esme come and stood at the door with me. She stood a while and I waited to hear what she had on her mind, for it was clear to me she did have something on her mind and was working up to saying it. At last she said to me,

Irie has not been an easy child to rear, you know, Bobby. She is not like our Miriam. Watching her teach you to read and write I have seen another side of her. Esme looked at me and smiled. You are good for her, Bobby. Daniel and I are grateful to you. She touched me on the shoulder, just a light touch of her fingers, and she said, I hope I am not embarrassing you now. I told her I was okay with it and I firmed my hat and stepped off the back step and went on down to the machinery shed and I stood in the shade and rolled a smoke. Standing there smoking my cigarette and looking out at the horses feeding in the paddock I was thinking about Irie and Esme and the surprising setup I had got myself into at the police house. I believe I was happier that morning than I had been since Dad passed on and our old way of life come to an end.

TWO

When the trouble started with Ben Tobin I was afraid there might
be no going back from it for Daniel and his family on account of
Ben's touchiness and Daniel's stiff way of dealing with people. It
was a pity there was no room in Daniel's dealings with the Mount
Hay people for a sense of humour. He just did not see things the
way we seen them. If that same trouble had come to George Wilson
he would have let it settle before jumping in, and feelings would
have worked themselves out so we would have soon been seeing
the funny side of it. But that was not the way it was to be.

The first we knew of it was when Rosie Gnapun come to the
kitchen door at the police house while we was having our breakfast.
Rosie said Ben had been beating the girl he had out there with

him at that place of his I helped him put up on Coal Creek. Rosie was the girl's auntie and I knew she hated Ben like bad water for beating her son one time. Rosie Gnapun knew how to hold a grudge and she never let go of it but lived to see it settled. She was just as bad as Ben at wanting to square accounts. Daniel did not know Ben Tobin and I did not tell him Ben was my friend. It was a dry time when Rosie come in with her report and I told Daniel he could get the jeep over Coal Creek and I guided him out there and watched him arrest Ben for assaulting Rosie's niece. Her name was Deeds.

Ben was not a big man but he was strong and quick as a snake. He had his own breed of pony that was just like him, stocky and reliable on their feet. Ben give me a wink and went along with the new constable as if it was not a problem for him to find himself being arrested. That young girl who was supposed to have took the beating off him was standing in the doorway. He kissed her cheek and told her he would be seeing her soon enough. I heard him say it. Daniel did not ask her nothing, which I remember as it surprised me. She did not look to me like a girl who was beaten. I thought Ben was planning something and I did not feel comfortable being along with Daniel if there was going to be trouble. Me and Ben had been mates since we was boys and if it come to it I knew I would have to be on his side. Daniel was wearing the handcuffs on his belt and that Webley revolver in its buckled-down holster that he got from George when George was handing over at the police station, but I do not think the sight of that gun was the reason for Ben being so easy about coming in with Daniel. I seen that in his crazy way Ben was enjoying being arrested. I come to this belief later that same day when I was lying on my bunk thinking about the way things had gone that morning, and worrying about how they was to go. Getting arrested was something that never happened to Ben before while George was the constable. I think Ben changed his mind about it later, but I believe he thought being arrested and going to gaol was something that was due to him, the way a reward of some kind is felt by other men to be their due. Ben had his own ideas about justice that few men shared with him. He was a hard man and I believe he thought a stint in gaol was a kind of respect that was owed him. That was the view I come to, which explained the quiet way he went along with Daniel when he could as easy have made a stand against him or got away into the scrub and Daniel would not have found him if Ben had not wanted to be found. I do not think Daniel would have understood Ben in a million years.

Ben pleaded guilty at his hearing and was sent to Stuart Prison in Townsville. I don't think he cared too much what he was accused of but just pleaded guilty to see the inside of Stuart, which he had heard a lot about, as we all had. Stuart would have been a holiday for Ben anyhow. It was the first time in Mount Hay we ever knew a whitefeller go to gaol for giving a black woman a hiding. But old Chiller Swales said it happened once before that he knew of. They let Ben out after a month and he come back into the country and was over at his place on Coal Creek again with Deeds like before, as if nothing had happened. My own private belief was that although Ben had gone to gaol without making a fuss he would not leave it alone now that he and the constable had something to settle between them. That is how Ben saw things. I knew him. He would want to settle up with Daniel Collins when he seen the advantage of doing it. Daniel Collins should have been watching out for himself from then on, but I believe he thought that episode was behind him. I had the feeling it was only just a beginning.

I went out to see Ben a couple of times but he never said nothing to me about his time in Stuart or his plans for getting his revenge on Daniel and I did not ask him about any of that. I knew if Ben wished to tell me something he would tell me without me questioning him. Deeds was not there when I visited him. But I knew it was not in him to let something like that rest.

Ben had a reputation for being tough that he had earned as a boy and a young man around Mount Hay. He did not have a lot of time for the boys of the town and he enjoyed taunting them just to show them how weak they was. Any offence he seen to himself, no matter how small it might seem to another man, was enough for Ben to be determined to have his own back and square it up. When he was out in the scrubs he was not like that. It was only something that come over him in the town. I never seen Ben do nothing by halves. Doubles was all he knew. If he hit you, you went down and you stayed down till he let you get up. I know what I am talking about. When we was not much more than boys and was mustering with our dads on the western boundary between Mount Heron Station and Long Ridge Hole, Ben stepped his horse on a dog at the lunch camp just to show off to the stockmen from them stations. The dog's leg was broken. I got down off my horse and I grabbed Ben's reins and I said him and me would no longer be friends. He stepped off and we had a fight. It was the only fight me and Ben ever had but it settled something. He told me afterwards he was sorry for what he done to the dog and I believed him and we made up and was better friends than we ever was before. When he was a youngster Ben had a well of cruelty his old man put in him with the beatings he give him as a child. Things could go either way with Ben, sweet and gentle or cruel. It was not easy to predict.

I did not say nothing about my thoughts on this to Daniel or to Esme, but I did think of telling them it was maybe time for them to leave Mount Hay and return to their quiet lives on the coast. What stopped me speaking out was my fear of losing Irie's friendship. I may even have said something to Irie, because she was always quick to see if I was brooding about something and she was not slow to speak her mind to me and ask me straight out. She would put her hand on my arm and look into my eyes with that serious look of hers and say, You going to tell me about it then, Bobby? And I always told her. On account of the trust we had between us.

Irie did not share everything that was between me and her with her mother and father. And I suppose that was another thing that was real but was not in the open, that sharing between us that me and Irie done without speaking of it. Having me eat with them in the kitchen of the police house brought me into their family in ways in the end that I do not think Esme give her attention to. But we can never see our future in the actions of today, except that we will know death one day as our parents knew death in their time. I could not let my mind believe in Irie's death. When she was teaching me, Irie took my hand in her own hand and shaped my fingers to the correct way of holding the pen. Now you try, she said and she watched and waited with patience for me to get it right. I lay on my bunk at night and looked out the open door of my quarters at the stars in the sky and I thought of Irie's hand guiding my hand. And in my thoughts I told my mother of my feelings for that girl and my mother understood my feelings, as I knew she always would.

. . .

Ben Tobin was the smartest bushman I ever knew, except for my dad. Ben was born and bred up by his dad in them Conway Ranges. He had mustered every inch of that wild country with his old man and mine when we was boys together. Our dads both took us out of school when we was ten years of age. Ben was two years ahead of me, which always made him seem a lot older than me and my superior, except when it come to horses, where I knew myself to be his equal. When I first arrived in the camps he was already handy and knew his way around the work. I cooked for the camp at first then mustered. I never met a bushman who did not know how to cook. We all done it when it was needed. Ben did the work of a grown man from the beginning. There was not a sweet spring of clear water in that hard-bitten stone country Ben Tobin did not know where it was by the time he was fifteen years of age. Even with his unsettling ways the stations liked having Ben around. He could get their wild cattle out of them springs when no one else could. Ben always treated me like I was his little brother. He stood by me.

A stockman come into Chiller's pub in Mount Hay from Brolga Station one afternoon. I do not remember the year. In those days we did not see many stockmen in town except at the end of the season. The stockmen was mostly blackfellers in those days and they stayed out on their country with their families during the wet. This feller was drinking in the bar and he looked at me and asked me what I was doing there. I had a very young look about me. Me and Ben was drinking overproof rum like we used to in them days. My dad and Ben's dad was sitting on the bench by the door outside smoking like they always did. They would get up and come into the bar to buy their next drink. We left our money on the bar in them days and Chiller took what was owed. My dad and Ben's dad never stayed inside any place if they could stay outside it. We took a bunch of old piker bullocks over to the railhead from Deception one time and Mr Dawson, who owned the place back then, offered to put us up in the house, but Dad and Ben's old man slept in their swags outside beside the ashes of the fire. And they never let me cook for them inside a house. They claimed inside spoiled the taste of food. Which is true. But I did not mind sleeping in a bed when I could get one. My dad smoked a pipe but Ben's dad rolled his own from them Champion plugs the stations used to buy in for their stores.

I did not think the stockman was being unfriendly but was just making conversation and asking after my reason for being there because he could think of nothing else to say and maybe he took me for a boy. I do not know. The mistake he made with Ben there was he put a kind of edge on his question to me, like he thought maybe I was stupid or should not have been there drinking overproof with the men. I did not take no offence from it. If he had known Ben Tobin that stockman would not have done that but would have known it might be going to cost him something. Anything out of the way when we was in town was like a spark to a can of petrol with Ben in them days. Ben went over to him and pointed back at me and he said in that stockman's face, taunting him in a singsong voice and making it rhyme, as if he was saying a line from a poem or a song, That's Bobby Blue you're talking to. And he dropped him. Ben had a fist like an iron ball. It was no good trying to hit him back. He was hard as wood all over and you would just bust your hand on him. The stockman was lying on the floor bleeding and Ben told him, If you get up I will kill you. I knew Ben was not serious about killing him but he made it sound serious the way he said it. He made the ringer crawl out the door on all fours, laughing at him all the way. When Ben come back in the bar no one said nothing to him, which was the way he liked it.

In them early days when we was not much more than boys it was like Ben had to keep proving for himself how weak other men were beside him and how they would take it from him, like he always had to take it from his old man, I suppose. I think I am the only man who ever loved Ben Tobin. But I did. And once you love someone you always love them. Dead or alive. It is not a matter of forgiving or understanding but of just loving. And that is in you, just as your memory of your mother is in you. You can do nothing about it, good or bad. Love is what it is. Just that. Call it by whatever name you like. Love is like faith. It does you good to have it, but it usually has a price to it.

It was no use asking Ben why he was doing something wild, so I never did ask him. It was like asking him why he was eating his breakfast or drinking his tea. He was just doing it because he was doing it. Just whatever come into Ben's head he would do it. No matter how wild it was. No one had ever gone up against him in Mount Hay and come off without being damaged and he pretty much had his own way in the town. It was before we had helicopters and it was all horses once you was off the tracks. That was what we knew. And that is where Ben was in his true home; in the scrub on a horse he was a quiet and reliable man you could depend on. But if someone who did not know him had a go at Ben for his cruelty he would take that man down off his horse and fight him. And he never let no one forget the beating he give them. There was an anger in Ben in them days that his dad put there with all the beatings he give him as a boy. I always feared he was going to kill a man one day. They still hung you for murder in Queensland and I did not want to see Ben Tobin hanged. I might curse him but my heart beat for him when he put himself in danger. And it is the heart that knows the truth in us. We can act as calm as you like, but the heart will betray us.

Ben never used a swear word that I ever heard. His dad beat him with the handle of his stockwhip close to killing him when he was a boy of five or six years of age after his dad heard him taking the Lord's name in vain, which Ben had picked up somewhere. Ben would not stand foul-mouthed people after that and we had plenty of them in Mount Hay, but they always cleaned up their tongues when Ben was around. I never knew him beat a woman or a horse so I was surprised when he owned up to beating that girl and went along with Daniel without making nothing of it at the time. I had my ideas, but I still knew there was some things I did not understand about that day and I was troubled thinking about them. Looking at Irie leaning over the kitchen table writing with her pen on them blue lines in the pages of her book it give me goose bumps knowing there was good and there was evil in this world and that any one of us can be touched by either any time without needing to get up and go looking for it. Now you try, Bobby, she said to me, and she handed me the pen, sitting up close so I smelled the child smell that was still on her.

THREE

They are lying up there behind the town dam in that stony cemetery, side by side like they was in life in them mustering camps all those years, next to my mother. The white ants cleaned up in no time the wooden crosses I planted. I replaced them crosses many times but I seen I was just feeding the ants and saving them fossicking for their own wood, so I quit replacing them crosses. They are still lying there, them two old fellers and my mother, unmarked just like the graves of all the poor of the world, but I know where they are. I do not know if white ants eat skeletons.

When Ben's dad died and Ben was no longer working the scrubs on a regular basis he took up that piece of ground out there at Coal Creek where Daniel Collins arrested him. I do not know that he ever bought that ground or if he was squatting on it. It was a dry flinty place and it suited him, cold as bones in winter with the wind coming up from the Moonlight Ranges with nothing to stop it. Like I said, Ben bred a tough-bodied type of pony on that piece of country with hard feet and never shod one of them. He would sell a horse if its feet turned out soft. He had a woman there with him from time to time but mostly he was alone with his horses or out in the country catching wild bulls or shooting brumbies or doing some other work for the stations, and on occasion he was stealing cleanskins and putting his own brand on them or someone else's who was paying him for them so much a head. Then he got Rosie's niece out there staying with him and that was the end of it for other women. Her name was really Deirdre, but she was always known as Deeds. She was not much more than a child. I do not believe Ben ever beat her but was gentle with her. When I was out there with them the first time, I seen Deeds had touched something in him he had kept hidden in himself till then. It was something gentle and private and too precious to him to be let out in the ordinary way. But it was there. It pleased me to see it.

The only work Ben refused for the stations was fencing. Wire strung in the bush was an evil to him and to all of us. Old wire neglected and grown over with the regrowth would cut your horse or bring you down. I often helped him cut the wire of an old fence and roll it up and hang it in the fork of a tree. Ben had a galley for his cooking out the side of his shack and cooked his meat in the open like his old man did and as I did for them when we was all working as a team back in the early days. When I was out there at his place on Coal Creek visiting Ben I smelled them good old cooking smells from our years together in the camps, beef fat falling onto the sandalwood coals and spitting. It is the only smell there is like that and for me it is the smell of home. Them days when me and Ben was boys and young men together in the scrubs with our old men and was trusted and respected. And all that was lost when our fathers passed on.

I did not know Deeds when she was first out there with Ben and only seen her that one time when Daniel arrested him, standing at the door of Ben's place looking on. It was her young age, I believe, that they sent him to Stuart for, for that and for Esme insisting to Daniel that it was his duty to protect the women of Mount Hay from brutal men. Esme had some ideas about it. She had a strong hold over Daniel in her opinions. I heard him call her The Reformer, like she was a horse that would buck him off if he didn't set the saddle on her just right. Daniel might have eased back and taken a bit of a look around if he had been left to himself to do his policing his own way, but you could see Esme was not going to leave him alone to do his policing his own way. She seen herself as part of the team. That was how she called it. Esme had an opinion about most things and it was not her way to keep her opinions in a back drawer. She said to Daniel, You are all that stands between these women and men like Benjamin Tobin. Esme was the only person I ever heard call him Benjamin. I might have said to her that she did not know Ben and never would know him but only knew the reputation he had made for himself when he was not much more than a boy and was given to wildness.

She was the identical same with their two girls as she was with Daniel. Esme liked to direct her family to her way of doing things, and she would direct people in the town too, but mostly they did not listen too closely to her after they got used to her. Them two girls, Irie and her sister Miriam, soon started sneaking off into the scrub on their own to get a bit of time away from their mother. She was always pressing them to be doing something useful every hour of the day. Esme was good to me and she pretty much left me to my own ways so long as she seen I was improving my reading and writing. She was firm on her family with the direction she wanted them to go in. I do not know if she was right to be the way she was or not. It is not mine to say. Them two girls of Esme and Daniel's was both of them pretty as spring robins, and they started looking for their own lives early in the piece as a result of Esme coming down on them the way she did. I seen they was starting to keep secrets from their mother, which they would not have needed to if she had trusted them. I never did keep no secrets from my mother. We knew each other's heart as we knew our own.

. . .

After Ben and me quit working the scrubs together and I got the job as the constable's offsider I was mostly around the police house and station from then on. The station and the house was all one timber building, and was most likely the best building in the town, the rest of them tin and fibro except for the hotel. The Catholic church was ripple iron and the Methodist chapel was never finished but was just the grey frame they begun with. That old frame always overgrown with wait-a-while vine since I was a kid. I do not know what happened to the Methodists. They most likely left or died.

Our mother was brought up by the nuns, which was where she got her education. She never knew her own family but always said to me and Charley, The nuns were my family. She loved the nuns and feared the priests. She and Dad met when she went out to the Holsons' place working as a governess to their kids and Dad was contract mustering for them people at the time. I got Bobby Blue from Mum and Dad being Mr and Mrs Blewitt. So Dad was always Blue ever since anyone could remember. They called us anything in them days. How you got the name that stuck to you was what you was called. So that is why I got Bobby Blue. And it was the name for me my mother liked best and she used it. My Bobby Blue, she said and looked at me like she feared a mountain was going to fall on me one of these days. I told her, It is okay, Mum. I know what I am doing and I can look after myself. But she felt something in her mind like a warning to her about her youngest boy and I seen that far-off knowing look in her eyes. Which she only had for me, like she sensed the terrible thing that was to happen lying out there waiting in the path of my future, like the serpent of the Bible waiting to turn the people to evil. She always wanted me to get an education but she would not go up against Dad's decision to take me out of school and I did not press her as I could not wait to get out in the camps with the men. I took hold of her and kissed her cheek and she trembled when I held her. She is with me until I go up the hill myself.

Them ripple iron and fibro buildings in Mount Hay was losing their nails from trembling in the winds, cold in winter, roasting in summer, expanding and shrinking and forever trembling. I was restless sleeping in a house that did not have a bit of a tremble in it. Rusting and slipping sideways off their stumps most of them was. Raised up in the forsaken highlands among the poison bendee and the bitter barks was how Chiller Swales said it. Godforsaken.

But Chiller only ever lived in Mount Hay. It was his old man built that pub.

It would have been a few months after Ben got back from Stuart Prison when the thing between him and Daniel broke out from sheer misunderstanding. We was all settled back into our quiet lives by then and was not thinking of Ben. If I am honest I would say I had begun to wonder if maybe I had been wrong about Ben needing to get his revenge. I still do not have no certainty of this. I could not read his mind and he did not speak to me of it.

It was one of them days when we was taking things easy. I had been washing my clothes after lunch and taking a long shower under the tank where we all did our washing. It was deep in shadow and always cool in there and I enjoyed the feeling of being clean and alone with myself and the job of washing out my shirts and moleskins, the chill of the tank water running over me and the smell of the soap. When I was changed into clean gear and had hung out my things to dry on the verandah over at my quarters I was called over to the house for afternoon smoko. Me and Daniel was in the kitchen of the police house drinking our tea and Esme was standing at the sink occupied with one of her domestic tasks. I watched Daniel drink from his tin cup. The tea was scalding hot. I seen he burned his lip on the cup's rim and he swore. I remember that day like I seen it on a film. Esme kept doing what she was doing at the sink, her back to the both of us. Daniel blew on the tea and sipped at it. I seen the way he heard the shuffle of the woman coming up to the back door but he did not make no sign of hearing her. Tip did not bark neither because she knew the woman from before. The woman called out something in that soft voice that made the hairs on the back of my neck stand up. Maybe she called, Mister Collins, but real soft, I did not exactly hear it. I knew who she was. It was like a cloud come over the sun at that moment.

Daniel twisted around in his chair and looked behind him out the screen door when the woman said her words. He must have seen a piece of the woman's yellow dress as she ducked away off to one side, just as I seen it from where I was sitting across from him at the table. I could have told him who it was but I said nothing. Things have a way of coming to you when you need to know them. There is no good ever comes out of rushing things before their time. The woman was down there at the side of the door where the shade still is beside the tank stand at that time of the afternoon. The side where Tip sheltered herself from the cold wind or from the hot sun, scrabbling a hollow for herself in that fine grey dust. Daniel kept twisted around in his chair looking out the door. I seen it then, the shadow of the storm coming up across the scrub, bending the sticks and humming through the silver grass. I remember there was the sound of the supply truck going away along the road, the sound strong then weak as it topped the ridges then ducked into the gullies. Fay Stubbs was new driving the supply truck then, which is why I remember hearing it. She had one of them Canadian Blitz trucks with an open-tray body that come in during the war. It had a winch and was the only vehicle could ever get over the creek crossings in the wet. You could hear the busted exhaust on that truck engine fading then coming back for hours in the silence, changing into low gear and grinding up them long ridges like nothing was ever going to stop it, eating the road gravel. I was thinking of Fay Stubbs going down the coast and having a good time like they say she always did, her fat arms wrapping the wheel, an unlit cigarette between her lips all chewed and wet where she was mouthing it. Hearing Fay's truck made me see the country in my mind, them long rolling ridges of scrub, one after another as far as the eye can see, going on into the haze of the day like a dream till you forget where you are. Just played-out mining and poor scrub country, that is all it is, fit only for them half-wild cattle and that was all the good it ever was. My country. I have no other.

Daniel was always on the lookout for some kind of mystery that he and Esme liked to talk about and that we did not talk about. I do not know what they meant by it. We talked about the struggle to get on, which is what we all had. Just our lives. If him and Esme ever seen them cock-horned beasts out in the bendee they would not think to speak of a mystery. Them cows never had one extra mouthful of feed in their lives. Their bones was scattered all over. It was hard country and the people in it was hard but good in their hearts and ready to share what little they ever had with each other. That is the way it always was for us in the ranges. If someone was in trouble the feuds was forgotten till they was helped. Then the feuds usually started up again.

Daniel swivelled back to the table from looking at the storm and he took up the last half-slice of toast from his plate and bit into it and he looked at the dirt under his fingernails. Like he had all day and there was no one asking for his attention. The salt of the tinned fish must have been stinging his burnt lip. Tuna in brine. We ate a lot of that. I had never had it before my days in the police house. I did not mind eating it. Esme was singing some song which I forget what it was. She was pounding at something on the board in time with her singing and I knew things was beginning, and I believe she did too in her own way, the song her way of covering up her feelings. That need in Ben to square things up, put there by his old man when he was a boy, exaggerating the hurt he had from his old man that had struggled to be healed in him till Deeds come into his life and loved him. I prayed for his healing. He was my friend.

I could feel the woman squatting in the dust by the tank waiting for Daniel. Her murmur and Esme's singing finding a sister rhythm, as if the two women was intending to harmonise their voices to make a hymn lamenting their lives. Which put me in mind of my mother singing her hymns in her dark beautiful voice, as if she was seeing eternity. Amazing Grace was my favourite, which I begged her to sing sitting by the stove. I seen the dew come in Ben's eyes listening to my mother singing that song when he was having a feed at our place one time, him cutting in real soft on that dinted old Hohner mouth organ of his and my mother smiling to hear the harmony of it with her own voice. My mother had a love of Ben. He said to me after we rode out to where the camp was in the morning, the mist still rising among the bendee, I did not know your mother could sing so well, Bobby. I knew Ben was not all cruel and I feared for him and what he might come to. If you heard him playing along with my mother on that old mouth organ you would know his sweetness too. I believe in his heart Ben always resented carrying that cruelness that had been put there.

Daniel took a deep drink of the tea. His chair creaked when he leaned back and Esme turned around. You going to see to her, then? she asked him, as if she was getting impatient waiting for him to do something. Daniel sat admiring his wife. I do not think I was hardly breathing, but was waiting for the thing to get going as I knew it would with these strangers from the coast. Esme's dark brown hair always brushed and shining, the strength of her features, her apron firm around her womanly figure, Daniel knowing her to be capable in her body and her mind, and maybe knowing her to be his better. You could see that. A determined woman, Esme was. She was not all bony and dried up like the women of Mount Hay but had a substance in her they did not have, or had lost. I never seen her smoke a cigarette and she did not drink. Daniel smiled to see her standing there in that blue and white cross-stitched apron of hers, pushing her hair off her face with the back of her hand and prompting him to his policing duties. I'm trying to finish this tea you made so hot I could hardly drink it, he said. Esme turned back to her task. And who complains it's never hot enough for him? was all she said. I could see they loved one another and I knew myself outside the true circle of that love but made welcome on terms of her generosity and concern for me as a young man without my own family. She was a mother and behaved like a mother and wished others to know the love of family. At that time I still liked to believe she was my friend.

Daniel drank the last of the tea and stood up. I stood up with him. Esme did not look around. The scald from the tea must have been severe in Daniel's gullet. I seen the face he made. He picked that new police slouch hat of his off the peg by the door and he brushed at it with his sleeve and put it on his head and went out and I followed him. My hat stayed on my head, where it always was. I said thank you for the tea to Esme and let the screen door bang to behind me, Esme's reply and the noise of the door together. That is my pleasure, Bobby, she said. I still hear that door banging to, rebounding and tapping twice against the old wooden lintel, a crack somewhere in that piece of timber that needed fixing.

. . .

Rosie Gnapun was sitting cross-legged in the grey dust in the shade beside the tank where the ant-lion larvae had their traps. Rosie's yellow dress was pulled down over her knees and she was rocking and drawing her private knowledge map in the dust with a twig. I went over and squatted down by the tank and Daniel squatted by her. Rosie's tears was making grey runnels along her black cheeks, her eyes pits of sorrow. Tip was watching from under the house, dewy-eyed and concerned, her jaw resting on her front paws. That dog was too soft-hearted to hunt. The white tip of her black tail was sweeping side to side on the dust like the windscreen wiper on Fay Stubbs' Blitz. I rolled a smoke and watched. I did not light my cigarette when I had made it ready out of respect for what Rosie would say.

Rosie looked at Daniel like she thought he should be ashamed of everything he had ever done and she said, They are gone,

Mister Collins. That is what has happened. They are not out there. You have let it happen to her again and that man has killed my Deeds. She sat looking at Daniel like she thought he had killed the child himself. And he looked back at her. I could see he was not understanding half of what Rosie was saying to him but was getting the message all the same, especially of her distrust of him. He was getting that clear enough. Daniel had a hard time with Rosie's mumblings and the way she hung her head and looked sideways at him and kept drawing with that stick in the dust while she was talking at him. It was like he was not the main one she was talking to but other people was present who was being witness to what she was saying and it was them she was really telling her story to, knowing they would be listening and understanding her and nodding their heads in sympathy. Them people me and Daniel could not see. I understood what Rosie was saying well enough without thinking about it or even trying to understand her. Her words was not always clear to me or to herself but her meaning was plain as can be. That is how my mother would have said it. Plain as can be. I hear her saying that.

Rosie said, He is laughing at you, Mister Collins. I seen Daniel heard this. I believe he had heard it before in the bar of Chiller Swales' pub and believed it to be true, even though it might have been no more than gossipy rumour. You put him in the gaol down there and they let him out again and now he has killed that girl. I've been out there and they are gone. Rosie give a loud wail and dipped her head onto her chest, that stick going deep into the ant-lion dust between her knees where she was making her secret patterns.

I looked at my unlit cigarette then I looked at the sky. I seen the black storm cloud had a touch of green in the depths of it. It was starting to block out the sun and I saw the light come on over at the Swanns' place and heard their lighting plant start up. The Swanns was a good family. They refused to go on the mains. I listened but could not hear the girls in the house and wondered if they was home yet. There was no sound coming from the kitchen. Esme's singing had gone quiet and I reckoned she was standing close by the screen door listening to Rosie. The girls should have been home about then. The storm was veering over towards Mount Dennison way over the other side of Coal Creek. The country changes over there and you get pockets of big timber and springs. The smell of the rain was in the air. The breeze cool and light on the dampness of my clean police shirt.

I forgot to wait and I lit my cigarette and drew on it, a small shudder slipping down my spine like the touch of a spider. I had to shift my feet. Tip raised her head at me and give a growl, like she thought I was about to do something fearful, her tail stilled. She was Esme's dog and no one else's at that time. I did not think she was much good for anything but sitting around the house watching over Esme and the girls. But I was to learn different. Esme would have had her inside if Daniel had allowed it. It was one point on which Daniel stayed put and had his way. I heard him reasoning with her one day in that quiet way he had that no one in Mount Hay ever let a dog in their house and the Collins should not be the first to do that. We must make some concessions to the local customs was what he said. But Esme would not have Tip put on the chain at night and she had her way with that. Which was to cost us all a great deal. I think if Esme had had her way she would have had everyone in Mount Hay thinking along her own lines about everything. The back step was it for Tip, but that dog never give up appealing to Esme's soft side and trying to get in the house with her.

When Daniel brought Ben in on that first occasion Tip went under the house and stayed there until Ben was taken down the coast. A dog knows. I do not know what Tip thought she saw in me at that minute when I shifted my feet under me but she seen something I did not see in myself and she objected to it. Just as a horse will see things its rider does not see. I take notice of the signs animals give us. They can save our lives.

Rosie give another howl like she had been wounded and Esme come out the door and she leaned down and lifted that old black woman under her arms and she held her to herself and comforted her, rocking Rosie back and forth like she was an injured child, even though Rosie was a big woman and heavy. But Esme had strength in her arms and she was young. Me and Daniel stood up and looked on at them two. Esme was looking over Rosie's shoulder at Daniel like she thought he had let down the family's good name. You would think Daniel had been slapped in the face. I seen he was not sure which way to go with it. I never heard Daniel lose his temper or get too excited, except on one occasion. He was always trying to keep things going along on an even level and reasoning his way with people. To my mind this was not always the best way to deal with things when a hard decision was called for. But it was Daniel's way and that is what he did. I do not think anything would have changed him. He had chosen policing for the adventure of his family coming out into the ranges and I do not think he was as well suited to the work as some people might have been. In the army, where he was a corporal, he had had to follow orders. Now he was called on to make the decisions himself. Which was different. I thought he looked to Esme too much of the time to take his orders. She was not the police, he was. I wondered if she always give him the full freedom of his job that he give her. But that is only my thinking and does not change how the tragedy of it worked out for us all in the end.

Esme was trying to coax Rosie into the house to sit a while with her but Rosie would not be coaxed and she eased herself out of Esme's arms and walked off. We three stood and watched her walking along the back way around the garden beds and over the tussocks and them big horse thistles, her bare feet scuffing the grey dust, as if she was reminding us we had missed out on the storms. As she went by it Rosie snapped a twig off the dead lemon tree Esme was always asking Daniel to root out and she went on out the side gate, leaving the gate open and calling out some words I did not hear. An old black woman's curse on Esme's house, I would say. On all of us. Cursing us. I went over and closed the gate before Yule's goats could get into what was left of Esme's vegetables. Them goats was out there on the road, heads up and watching for their chance, a young kid bleating for its mother's tit and getting kicked for its trouble. Yule and his wife and their own tribe of young ones would be roasting that little feller shortly, and if the wind was right we would get the smell of it at the police house. When I come back from closing the gate I seen Esme had not held off from speaking her mind to Daniel.

Daniel had read me from his geology book one evening that the grey dust of the ranges is all that is left of what was once mountains now worn down by time. I thought of that when I seen Rosie's bare feet scuffing through it. Rosie was the grey dust herself. It was something to watch out for and I always give her my full respect, as my father did. Them Old People knows things us whitefellers can never know. They are the dust of them worn-down mountains themselves and the knowledge is in them like the marrow of their souls. Which it will never be in us. We are like germs to them Old People, blown in on a foul wind. I knew that from Dad.

. . .

Me and Daniel went down to the yards and I brought the horses in and we checked their shoes. We did not talk about Rosie and her visit and I did not ask Daniel what he had in mind to do about Ben. I thought it best to let him settle and if he needed my advice he would ask me for it. When we had done with the horses I filled the fuel tank on the jeep and checked the oil, then we went into the police office and took the guns out into the scrub for some shooting practice. Daniel had the top-break Webley left him by George Wilson and I had the .303. We did not take George Wilson's old twelve-gauge shotgun that was kept in the kitchen. It was an old gun and the right hammer would hook into cock but would usually misfire. George had used the left barrel for shooting snakes if he seen one up close by the kitchen door. He did not mind if they went under the tank. There was always frogs there in the cool.

Me and Daniel sighted our weapons up and I took some shots with the Webley at a line of empty tuna in brine tins we set up. I knew it was not easy to hit anything with a revolver as I had often had a go with Ben's old Colt what he bought off an American soldier who stayed behind in Townsville like a lot of them Yanks did after the war. Ben always carried that gun in a closed holster tied to a dee on his saddle with a strap of redhide. He shot cancer-eyed bulls with it mostly. We cut them old bulls open while they was still hot and put strychnine powder through their meat for the dingoes. I was a clean marksman with a .303 as I had used my dad's rifle for years shooting brumbies and dingoes whenever there was not a lot of station work going. I made good money with that rifle. You could get them guns for one pound each then. There was any amount of army stuff around after the war and it was cheap. Our own stuff and American. Everyone had something. The bounty on dingo scalps was one pound one shilling each and the tail and mane hair of the brumbies was three shillings and sixpence a pound. Norm Barry made a good living at it. That is all Norm ever did his whole life. We used to see him once or twice a year. The rest of the time he was out in the escarpments with his packhorses and his gun horse. I did not know what he ate but when he come into town he just drank rum over at Chiller's place till his funds run out. He never had much to say. Ben's dad was the only person Norm Barry ever had anything to say to. Him and Ben's dad had known each other since they was boys. The ranges was all either of them ever knew. I do not believe either of them had ever been down to the city in their life.

I seen Irie coming out to where me and Daniel was shooting. I said, Irie's coming. Daniel give a start, like I'd scared him, and he looked around and watched her come up to us. He was not at ease in himself since Rosie's visit. He asked Irie what the trouble was. She said there was no trouble and could she have a go with his handgun. Daniel said, I don't suppose it would do you any more harm than it does us to know how to shoot a gun. He showed her how to hold the revolver and she took a shot at the cans and missed. She flinched away from the blowback of powder, which he had not mentioned to her and she was not expecting it. She would not touch the gun again after that. She give me a look I did not like and turned around and went home rubbing at her eyes. I lined up a target on an old-man bottle tree a hundred yards off and shot off three rounds with the .303. I hit the centre of the target with all three. There was no adjustment needed to the sights. I hit two cans with the Webley. Two out of six did not seem too bad to me with that handgun. We cleaned the guns in the office and when we got back to the house Esme was ready to serve up.

She set Daniel's plate of food in front of him and said, So who are you planning on shooting, Daniel? She called him Daniel when she was displeased with him about something. Irie said, Daddy didn't hit any cans, Mum. Daniel did not say nothing to this remark but just laughed and give Irie a look. She give him a cheeky grin and I seen the love in her eyes for him that was fighting against her fear of being disappointed in him. I realised then that she wanted her dad to be a hero. I knew Daniel had been a hero in New Guinea fighting the Japs and I promised myself I would tell Irie that when the moment come for it. But I always forgot and never did get to telling her. Daniel was one of them men who do not big-note themselves and a kid might easily think he was nothing special. They left the talk of shooting at that. I did not ask Daniel if the police induction he had down there on the coast ever included instruction in using the sidearm. He had told me something of his time in New Guinea, but only that he was made a corporal. I seen for myself he was at home handling the .303 and hit the target on the bottle tree with a fair degree of accuracy, so perhaps he was an ordinary infantry soldier and had used the rifle before. That is the way it seemed to me. But I do not know for sure. He never talked to me about the details of his time in the army. It was Esme first told me he had come out of the army before going into the police service. She was proud of what he done fighting up there in the jungles. She said to me once with a kind of sadness in her voice, Heroes are always shy men. Isn't that true, Bobby? I did not know if it was true or not so I said nothing to it. But I seen how her eyes was filled with emotion for him. I do not believe she expected a reply from me anyway, but just needed to tell someone her love for him.

We sat eating our meal of corned brisket and potatoes, the steam rising off the pink meat. Just as my old dad, I liked nothing better than to eat the yellow fat on corned meat while it was hot, the thicker the better, with that bubbly look about it. But Daniel and his family cut the fat away from their meat and left it on the side of the plate. Irie had a go at it when she seen I was enjoying it but she did not take to it. Tip's nose was at the door and she give a bit of a whimper every few minutes, imploring them to toss her the fat. To my way of thinking, in that house the dog got the best of it. The beans and carrots from Esme's garden that she had kept in the chiller was green and orange on our plates. They had been kept awhile and tasted of mould. But Esme's bread was the best I ever tasted next to my mother's. She made it herself.

Miriam said, Jon Swann hit me for nothing. Esme said, Did you cry? I hit him back like Daddy tells us to, the girl said. You shouldn't go hitting people, Esme said. Daniel reached and touched the girl on the shoulder. Jon Swann won't hit you again, darling. Bullies don't like getting hit back. Irie said, Miriam is lying, Dad. Jon Swann is not a bully. He did not hit anybody. Esme leaned down at her youngest. Is this true, Miriam? He hit me, the child said. Irie don't know everything. He did not hit you, Irie said in her quiet voice, stating the fact in a way that was not unlike her dad's manner of talking, so that we all believed her and disbelieved Miriam. *Doesn't* know everything, Esme said, correcting Miriam's way of speaking. I knew that already and me and Irie give each other a quick look. That is when Miriam started to cry. Now come on, eat up, you two, Esme said. I *am* eating up, Miriam shouted through her crying. Like a bird she was, quick to fly. Esme put a hand to the little girl's cheek, as if she was testing for a sign of fever, and I thought of my mother's hand against my cheek and her words of comfort to me that was also a warning. We all hang on the cross, Bobby Blue. And I seen how Miriam was suffering the injustice of the entire world just then, the way children will. On the cross, she was. Daniel wiped the gravy from his plate with a slice of Esme's soft white bread and ate it, taking it in two mouthfuls. He picked up his mug and washed the sodden bread down with tea. There's more, Esme said, looking at him. She waited for him to look at her but he did not look at her, so she got up and started clearing away, telling the girls to go and wash and get themselves ready for bed. Irie went over to Miriam and she put her arm around her sister and took her out to the tank where the washing things was kept. I heard Miriam say, He did hit me. But her need to be believed had gone out of it.

. . .

The children was in bed and blue lightning was flickering over behind the high ridge of Mount Dennison. The back door was open to the warm night, the thunder faint, just like the rumbling of the ore train we had in Mount Hay when I was a boy. Esme said, What are you going to do, Dan? It was Dan now. Daniel was twisted around in his chair watching the lightning out the door, a book open in his lap. I rode those Mount Dennison bluffs and stony ridges with my dad and Ben and his dad many times. There was wild bulls in there that never seen a man in their whole lives and had no fear of us when we come on them but only a blind belief in their own great strength, as if they was gods. If they was old, Ben's dad shot them between the eyes with that Colt. They shook their heads when they was hit with that big slug and they looked at Ben's dad with a calculating surprise and they only dropped to their knees when they took the second shot. I always felt sorry for them and how they had lived up there without men for all their lives since they was dropped from their mothers. Ben's dad said killing them was a mercy. But I did not see it.

I watched the lightning with Daniel. He did not answer Esme at once. I thought of the quiet patience my mother had. Then the day come when she saw her answer looking at her. Do not ask, you will know when you need to know, she said. That is the way she always understood it. My mother had foreknowledge with her faith. That was Daniel and Esme's mystery if they wanted a mystery out in them ranges, but no one was ever going to talk to them about those things. Those things was private to all of us who lived out there, if we was religious or not. We never spoke about them things, not even to each other. We just knew them. People from the coast would not understand. People like the Collins knew the city and the coast and they had another way of seeing things that was not our way of seeing things. The Collins wanted to know what they had no need to know. There was no respect in them for the mystery they hoped to entertain themselves with. They was not bad people, just ignorant. My mother said the ignorant was to be pitied, not despised.

My mother loved them nuns that looked after her with kindness and great care when she was a child. They were my family, she told me, and that far-off look come into her eyes as she thought of them, naming them and considering her memories of them, the sisters

she called them. She was knitting by the stove and me and Dad
was home one time when it was too wet to get about the country.
She told me she had never forgotten the first night she was with
the nuns. I think Dad had heard the story before but did not mind
hearing it again, as I seen he was listening with his eyes on my
mother. She must have decided I was old enough just then to hear
her story and to keep it inside myself. My mother was an orphan.
Like everyone, she said, I must have had a mother and a father,
but I do not remember them or know anything about them or if I
had brothers and sisters. I always thought they was dead, she said.
The Mother Superior was standing out the front of the hall on a
platform with some of the other nuns that first night and everyone
was assembled before her listening to her. My mother was standing
out in the body of the hall with the very young kids and her legs
suddenly give way under her and she went down in a heap on the
floor. Everyone turned around and looked at her. Her legs had lost
their power to lift her back up and she stayed down, crumpled and
helpless as a shot cat, the whole assembly staring around at her and
the kids nearest to her moving back a little to give her room, and
maybe in fear of her. The Mother Superior was the boss of the place
and she stopped giving her speech when she seen my mother go
down and she stepped off the platform and walked along the middle
of the hall and she bent down and picked my mother up from the

floor and cradled her in her arms and carried her back out of the hall and into her own room up on the top floor of the building.

The Mother Superior put my mother in her own bed and she pulled the covers up around my mother and she leaned down and kissed my mother on the forehead. I have never lost the feeling of that kiss, my mother told me, and she looked into the firebox of the stove as she said it, her knitting forgotten between her fingers, as if she was seeing a vision of herself as a child in the Mother Superior's bed that first night in the convent. And the Mother Superior said to her, Do not be afraid, my child. We will take care of you. You will get well and strong again with us. And that is what happened. It is a true story. My mother's legs got their strength back and she was always made a fuss of by the nuns after that. They saw in her recovery the work of their faith in their Saviour, the Lord Jesus Christ. And they give my mother special lessons and she was taught to play the piano and to speak French. That is how she come to be a governess on that station when my dad was out there mustering that time, which is when they met up and fell in love.

That story must have reminded my dad of his first meeting with my mother out there on that station. The name of it slips my mind just now. When she finished telling her story he got up off his chair and he come over and rattled the fire up then he leaned and kissed my mother on the cheek. My mother always sung her songs, mostly hymns but not all of them. She had a lovely voice until the last. She was not old when she died. I do not know what she died of. It was sudden and come without no warning while we was out mustering.

. . .

You hear me, Daniel? Esme said. I am talking to you. Daniel looked up at her and he said, I do not know what I will do about Ben Tobin. I must give it some thought. He picked up his empty cup off the table and looked into it, turning it to one side to see the pattern the leaves had left. Esme said, If that girl is dead, Daniel Collins. Like it was a warning to him. He looked at her, and I seen the hurt in his eyes. Please do not say that, Esme. I will go out and look for them in the morning. We do not know yet what has happened. We only have Rosie's word for it. And he looked at me and he asked me what I thought. I seen he was really asking not just what I thought but what I thought he should do. I said Ben would take some finding in the scrubs if he did not wish to be found. And that is all I said. I got up and said goodnight and went on out to my quarters. I feared we was going to have trouble with Esme pushing at Daniel the way she did.

I did not wish to listen to their conversation any longer. Like most men, or all of us, Ben was a mixture of things in himself.

I did not know everything there was to know about him, that is for sure, and I hoped not to misjudge him. We change from what we was. There was changes in me and there was changes in Ben as we grew from boys to young men, and as time went on we thought things we had never thought before and did things we had never done before. Which is one reason I disliked to hear Esme and Daniel judging on Ben. I do not think Ben himself ever really knew what he was going to do in advance of actually doing it. Deeds had softened him, and maybe he was going to let it slide this time. It would be a first for him if he did. But so what? I do not know the answer of it to this day. If I could ask Ben right this minute I believe he would wink at me and play a few bars on that old Hohner of his. And that would be my answer. Esme and Daniel wanted things clear cut. But there wasn't no clear cut with Ben.

As I was going out to my quarters along the path I seen Irie and Miriam scooting off along the track past the chook house, which Esme called the hen run. Shadows of children in the moonlight. I took off my clothes and lay on my bunk and a picture of Irie come into my head and I let myself think about her while I smoked a cigarette. The day I heard my mother died, standing up there at the yards beside my dad, I knew then I was going to die one day myself. Before my mother died I never thought of the death that was waiting in me and always believed I was going on forever.

I had a fear for them two children and could not imagine Irie's death but only had the fear of it, like she was my own child. She must have been around twelve by then and a real young woman, serious and full of feelings. I valued the friendship I had with her very highly. I do not have words for it.

FOUR

The track ahead of the jeep was not evident with all the rain they'd had over that way and the heavy new growth of wiregrass. Daniel weaving around this way and that through the stands of bendee and prickly Moses. He said a number of times he could not remember the track from last time, speaking his words low and half mumbling, as if he was talking to himself, the jeep leaping and rattling. But I knew what he was saying just by the look of him, leaning over the wheel and gazing around as if he thought he was going to see a signpost out there in the scrub saying, COAL CREEK THIS WAY. But there are no signposts in the scrub and only the scrub itself. There is all the signs you need if you are only looking for them and wish to see them. I told him I knew the road and it was there in front of us and I indicated the direction. He was nervous and keyed up with everything that was in his mind and not knowing what he was going to do. I seen water in some old ruts of Fay Stubbs' mail truck fifty yards over to our right from the last time she went through, the glint of white sky in a long pool. But I did not point it out to him.

It was not one track out to Coal Creek but many tracks. The trick was to pick the right track on the day. It is the general direction you must take in that country once you are off the made road, not one particular track. I do not know what Daniel saw in the scrub ahead of him that day but I do not think his mind was clear on the general direction he was going in. It seemed to me he was distracted thinking of Esme's way of pushing him to his duty and was fraying somewhat with the irritation of that, like an old rope wearing thin rubbing against something and getting ready to snap next time you put a sudden strain on it. I wish he would have told her he was the police not her and got that settled between them. I never heard my mother tell my father the way he should go with his own work and I never heard him tell her how to do her work neither. No good can come of telling other people how to do what they are supposed to be doing of their own. But only irritation. I seen it before with Chiller's missus before she died. Chiller grieved for his wife when she was gone, but all the same he was like a man on holiday, though he was too ashamed to admit it. You could not miss it. There was no one tailing him.

If Daniel had asked me to drive I would have got us to Coal Creek without troubling myself too much about how to get there or anything else, except I knew we was not going to get to Coal Creek that morning in the jeep. The storm was over that way and the creek would be too high. I knew that. But he did not ask. I was not happy that morning sitting up there beside Daniel in that police jeep when I knew we should have taken the horses. I never had no trouble working for my dad alongside Ben and his dad. There was never one of us telling this or that to nobody else about how to get the job done. I did not mind working under a boss, but I was fraying a bit too with Daniel's way of half doing things his way and half doing them Esme's. He was never sure of what he was going to do and when things did not work out for him he was cursing at being given the wrong advice by his wife. And none of this out in the open but all rancid inside him. It made me feel like a dumb idiot sitting up there next to that man, and I did not like it and was not easy with him or with myself. What we was doing going out to Ben's place was not clear to me. I always liked to be clear about what I was letting myself in for.

. . .

The scrub was swaying and heaving with strange unsettling shadows that morning, the wind not knowing which way to blow after the fuss of the storm passing through in the night. There was unusual shapes of high cloud, belled and bowed like they was under some pressure from below and could not move on, left over from the violence of the storm like people left behind to settle up on a violent dispute. Flocks of crows diving and cawing and crying out through the tops of the red ash pines, which some call the soap tree, agitated and angry with us for disturbing them, and unhappy with the day for their own reasons, which I did not know. But I do know it is the white eye of the crow rules that country of the birds and they was telling us something they knew that we did not know. Them are the kind of signs the bush gives you. But Daniel was not reading the signs that was there, and was too busy looking for the signs that was not there. And maybe that was like me with not reading the alphabet before Irie took me in hand, and Daniel did not know how to read them signs that I was bred up with, and it was his ignorance on top of everything else that was frustrating him now. I would not say Daniel was angry exactly but he was not far off it. He was a foreigner in our country and was not comfortable knowing he might make a mistake any time. And maybe it takes a bigger man than Daniel Collins ever was to call out for help or to admit to being unsure of himself. That is what I believe. But he did not ask me nothing, only went on as if he knew enough already, when I could have told him the way of things in the scrubs, just as Irie told me the way of reading and writing and I was happy to learn from her. I believe Daniel thought he had nothing to learn from me except the gossip of people around the town, which was something I did not care about and I knew little of it.

In my dream in the night I had seen Rosie's knowledge map and I had a sweat of fear in the dream of Rosie going up against me. I was afraid of what that old woman was up to. Her map was gone in the morning when I went out to shower myself, the ant-lions' cone traps built back up in the night, like them insects never give up. People from the coast like Esme and Daniel did not believe that the Old People of that country have their own way of writing and reading with knowledge maps, but think there is only their own alphabet to read by. Which was their arrogance. But them Old People always had their own way of writing that was kept secret from the whitefeller. I could not read it but I knew they had it.

Just after we turned off the made road at the ten mile outside Mount Hay earlier, when the mist had not gone off the country yet, I seen a yellow robin in a patch of mesquite, the native bird sitting in the branches of the stranger bush. That bird did not fly when we rattled past her in the jeep but stayed put and I thought

about her sitting there. Which was another sign to me. The ant-
lions and Rosie's people are kin to the ranges. Everything abides
in them. The beauty of their persistence awed Daniel Collins, his
mind aching for a connection to the mystery that would make
him certain of something in himself. I seen he had formed a kind
of love for the country but doubted his own presence in it. Daniel
was to die a stranger in that country that had not formed him but
had bewitched him like a story bewitches a child and the child
cannot sleep thinking on the story after its mother has put out
the light and gone to her own bed, but goes on dwelling in that
country of the witch and the fairy, fearing the end for itself in the
story. I believed I understood that morning that nothing of Daniel's
longing was to be satisfied in him. For he was longing in the wrong
direction. He was looking to understand something that could
not be understood. It was not understanding was missing in him,
but knowing. Like Rosie knew. Like the ant-lions knew. Like that
yellow robin and them angry crows all knew. Daniel Collins seen
understanding as the way to the comfort of his troubled soul, but
anyone could have told him he was on the wrong track with that.

The day was warming up and I took off my jacket and tossed
it into the back. It was Ben brought me that jacket back from
Townsville when he was there at the meatworks getting away
from his dad for a spell that time. It was leather with a sheepskin

lining and I always wore it on cold mornings. Daniel told me my first week with him I should be wearing the police-issue jacket but I said I would not be hanging up my old jacket and he seen I meant it. The great wedgetail eagles was circling already, rising on the thermals like gods themselves into their own blessed sky, their distant cries pitching across the wind. God's eagles. The eagles of Christ. Lord Jesus Christ and his blessed eagles. The talons of the Lord. It was my mother's voice in my head telling me her own feelings of unease. My mother always come near me when I was in trouble. In her death too she was my mother. I took her belief of gentleness and it come into me and stayed with me. I did not like being with Daniel if we was to meet up with Ben, and I was wishing I could have gone out to Coal Creek on my own and talked to Ben and been just the two of us. I knew me and Daniel was not going to make it in the jeep out to Ben's place anyway. After that storm the creek would be running a banker this morning and not even that old Blitz of Fay Stubbs' would have got across.

But Daniel would have to learn the country his own way if he was ever to learn it. If he had asked my opinion that morning, nice and casual, the two of us men together, smoking a cigarette and looking at the weather, I would have told him. But he did not ask. And he did not smoke neither. He just backed the jeep out of the shed first thing after breakfast before it was scarcely light and told me, Get in, Bobby, like I was his dog and had nothing of worth to say. He was wearing George Wilson's top-break Webley in that closed holster, which did not help my feelings one bit. Daniel's face just as closed and set as that beat-up holster of George's. I did not think there was no need for it. We had the .303 behind the seats on a pile of sugar bags. We always carried that rifle when we went out in the jeep so I did not think nothing about it being there. Sometimes there was animals needed to be shot.

When we was leaving the police house Tip come out and barked at us. Esme standing at the back door watching, the tea towel in her hands like a flag, red and white, but not waving it, seeing to it that her man did not spend another day thinking on what he might do but was going out to get it done before the sun was up. My mother always said everything means something. I seen Daniel had put the tucker box in the back, which cheered me up somewhat, as I guessed Esme would have packed it for us and her packing of provisions was always generous. Esme did her own job well. I never heard no one complain to her about it nor have a reason to. Which made me wonder why she did not leave others to get on with their jobs on their own but had no confidence in anyone but herself to get things done right. I looked at her one evening with the thought of asking her this. I must have looked at her for a long time because she laughed and said to me, My goodness,

Bobby, what are you thinking? I said I was not thinking nothing and I went back to copying out the book me and Irie was doing. I do not think Esme would have had an answer for me if I had asked her that question. I do not know what she thought I had in my mind staring at her like that.

I was away with these thoughts when Daniel suddenly pulled up and turned off the motor. He did not speak but sat looking into the scrub ahead of the jeep where the track cut through a stand of sandalwood. We called it the bush plum. Sitting there staring as if he seen someone riding towards us out of the scrub. The answer to the things he was trying to understand in what he was seeing. But I do not think Daniel Collins was a man to ever see things that was not there. Which was his loss. The track was grown over with wiregrass from them late storms they had been catching over that way, but it was there. There was nowhere else for it to be but there. The engine block ticked and just then the wind dropped and the sudden stillness settled over Daniel Collins and me, the pair of us sitting there in that ex-US army jeep side by side out there in the scrub. I did not know where this was going to get us to. The stillness of the bush. That is it. Daniel sitting and looking. A puzzled man out there. In the hand of the mystery. Cupped and held until the day of his death, as we all are, like my mother as a helpless child held in the arms of the Mother

Superior, safe so long as them arms of that kind woman held her. The sisters was my family, she always said. She knew herself to have been cherished.

Daniel spoke suddenly into the quiet, the cries of the eagles faint now, rising in their circles. He said, Esme asked me last night what did Rosie say exactly that Ben did to the girl. He was silent a minute and I felt I was not expected to answer what he had said so I waited until he spoke again. Which he soon did. I could not talk to Esme about my feelings, he said. I told her Rosie just drew it in the dust. She did not say it. She could not say it. Esme said to me, Are you going to tell me or not? I can't tell you, I said to her. The thought of the abomination of it has silenced me. The hideousness of evil cuts deep in us. But Esme would not leave it at that. Can't or won't, Daniel Collins? she said.

Was he speaking to himself or to me? I wanted to ease my left foot which was pressed up against the side of the metal guard, but I did not dare to move even one muscle in my entire body. Something was coming out of him. Esme is a strong woman and I thank God for her presence in my life, he said. She waited for me to come back from those cursed jungles up in the north and I knew how much she believed in me. The war was a test for both of us. But it was a clean test. We knew where we stood with the war. After I came back we were closer than we had ever been before I went. I did not expect this job to be something that would come between us and prove difficult up here in the ranges. But that is how it has turned out. Daniel did not look at me while he was speaking but looked straight ahead into that stand of broken sandalwood, shattered and twisted by dry heat and winds over the years, looking into it as if he was talking to someone I could not see who was in there. It unsettled me. He said, I told her, I do not hate Ben Tobin and I do not wish that man harm, but I will find out what he has done to the girl. Esme would not leave it and she said, But you would hate him if he was ever to touch one of our girls. It upset me to hear her say that as I knew it was bringing something into this thing with Tobin that did not rightly belong in it. Daniel stopped speaking and was silent a long time after this.

I wanted to roll a cigarette but thought I would wait until he got out what he was needing to say. I felt, he said, as if Esme was cheating when she said that, bringing our girls into it. He turned and looked at me then as if he suddenly remembered I was with him. I looked back at him and I seemed not to be able to stop myself from blinking. So I pretended to cough and put my hand up to my mouth and turned my face aside. He said, It upset me and I could not settle to sleep after that. I told her Ben Tobin is not going to touch our girls. That is not the issue for us. That is not going to happen and you should not speak of it as if it is something else for us to worry about.

I did not know what I could say to this, so I said nothing.

The eagles was black specks way up there in the dazzle of the sky, like specks in my eyes, then gone, the pair of them, circling each other in great looping rings, wings fixed and still. The dance of the eagles. In my eye then gone then back again in my eye as if they could make themselves disappear and appear again, mesmerising their prey with the magic of themselves a thousand feet above the country. Was I no more than a black speck in the eye of the eagle? The air was so heavy with moisture it should have held them to the ground. How do they rise without effort into the white emptiness of sky like that without no weight on them? I have often seen a pair of them perched close to the ground and giving me that superior look they have, and I have come on them stripping a carcass and they have looked up at me sitting my horse and I have seen their resentment of my presence. Which is surprising, but you see it when you come close to them, or if you have shot them and hung them spread on a fence as some people will. That is something I have never done, to shoot an eagle. I would fear the curse of it would never leave me in peace ever again. But people do it. Calm as anything. Like they believe they are the boss of the eagles. Which they are not. I could not do it. An eagle is an eagle. We are not that.

We are only men. When you live as we had lived our lives in the scrubs you know you are not the boss of nothing and there is the sky and the eagles and the scrubs going on forever into them great stone escarpments. No man knows himself to be the boss of that.

Daniel started the motor and drove on, easing his way through the tormented landscape. I had said nothing. We saw bones. Daniel pointed them out like he thought I might not have seen them. I knew them bones belonged to an old scrubber bull my dad shot fifteen years before. Some years after he had shot that big old bull we hung the skull in the fork of a dead cabbage gum, my mother called them blue gums. There was a great spread of horns on that skull. It had been missing some years already. The horns on that old bull was the widest I ever seen. Some gold fossicker must have taken that skull to sell it. And no doubt he boasted about it to his friends. The hole my dad's bullet made was dead centre of that skull, looking at you, like an eye, looking at you out of the death of that old bull. It would have give Rosie a turn to see it.

. . .

The cut of the track down the bank of the creek to the wattle flat was right there in front of us and Daniel just kept going. I grabbed the handhold under the windscreen and I said, Hold up there, Daniel! He stomped on the brake as if my voice woke him from a dream. The wattle flat was flooded by the rush of the creek, the wattles bent over, sticks and rubbish caught up in them bowed branches going with that heaving current. I do not think we can go through there, I said. But I had no need of saying it. He asked me, Is there some way across for us? I indicated with my hand and told him, On the horses we can ford lower down where she flattens out over the stones, but the bank down there will not take this vehicle. She's a breakaway where the flat was all washed out by that big flood ten years ago. You will not get a vehicle over there without grading the bank. If you give an hour or two the horses would make it.

Daniel switched off the motor and stepped down and went up to the edge of the cut and stood looking down the bank at the brown flow of the water. I got out and went over and stood beside him. The sun was striking through the tops of an old budgeroo, what they call mahogany tree, on the other side of the creek. I knew that tree at the crossing from when I was a boy. It had not changed one bit and my dad would have known it today. There was not many of them mahogany trees around just there and this old man stood alone. A faithful pair of black cockatoos was watching us from the top branches of the budgeroo, waiting to see what we was going to do, like our arrival at the crossing had disturbed them at their lovemaking.

Daniel said, Why don't we boil up and have a drink of tea before we head back? He was calmer now. The tension gone out of him. The creek was stopping him and that must have been clear to any man. The creek was making his decision for him. He did not seem to care a whole lot about the eventual outcome of this any more. I still did though. He considered me for some time and I was afraid he might be going to ask me something about what I thought of the way he spoke to me about Esme and was maybe regretting letting me into his private thoughts like that, which I had not asked to be let into. I stepped away and went around to the back of the jeep and picked the axe out of its divot and went over and took a swing at an old dead piece of sandalwood and I hit it hard with the back of the axe. The splinters flew and I heard one pinging past my ear. A splinter of sandalwood went into the eye of a young Chinese boy who used to work for Chiller at the pub and the boy was blind in that eye from then on.

I got a fire going and went over and dropped the rear of the jeep and slid the tucker box out and opened her up. Esme had wrapped sandwiches and a big piece of her fruit cake. I loved that fruit cake of Esme's. I squatted down and set the billy on the flames and fed sticks all around it. I smoked a roll-up and squatted by the fire watching the water heating, bubbles hissing around the edge of the billy, the smell of the smoke and my tobacco. It was the smell of old times. Daniel was standing across the fire from me. He said, I should not have spoken like that to you about Esme. I stayed squatted down and poked a dry stick in under the billy and squinted into the smoke. It was blowing over me the way smoke from a fire always will blow over you. The morning was more than half gone. The sound of the creek roaring. I liked to hear the roar of a creek in flood. It was the sound of the country breathing after a long dry spell of holding its breath. That is how it always seemed to me, as if the country was letting it all out in a rush. There was a happiness in that sound that would have made my mother want to dance.

The black cockatoos got tired of waiting for us to leave and took off, keening their dismal cry like they just lost a friend, flapping them big black wings of theirs lazily and showing us the red flash of their tails like they was sending us messages. I was glad to be out in the scrub away from the police house. Daniel said no more and I thought maybe his silence was a sign he was listening for once. The bush is always talking to us. The water boiled and I tossed in some leaves and lifted the billy off the fire with a stick and set it on the ground to one side, steaming and strong with the smell of the tea. I tapped the sides of the billy to settle the leaves and turned to Daniel. He handed over his quart pot and I filled it and handed it back to him. He cut the cake and squatted across from me and we sipped our scalding tea and chewed the cake and looked into the fire with our own thoughts. I always liked a fire. I was the one got out of my swag first thing in the old days with Dad and Ben and his dad, and it was me who always got a fire going and a billy heating up and doing something about our breakfast, which depended how long we'd been out in the camp. Being up first before it was light and the white mist was still rising among the timber. The times I seen a big old man roo standing there watching us, like he was wondering if he might come up and introduce himself. I used to wait till I had the fire going well and the billy on before I went off a little way into the bush and had a long satisfying pee, the horses clinking about in their hobbles, heads raised watching me. I often told them my dreams. I did not speak to the others about my dreams. And the old man roo watched me pee and scratched himself behind his ear and he turned around and hopped away real slow, shaking his head and thinking about the show he had seen out there in his country, the men and their fire and the man peeing and talking to himself. That was our life. I seen it many times in them big cow eyes of the roo, soft and dreamy with that easy wisdom of his country in his long head. Ben liked to drink his tea while he was still in his swag and I was happy to take it to him. I went over to where he was sleeping and pulled back that grey blanket of his with the red stitching around the edges of it, and I crouched there looking at him, watching him waking up and smelling the tea and opening his eyes and seeing me there. Tea boy! he said, and he smiled and reached his hand out for the quart pot. Are we getting some of that toasted damper of yours? Ben Tobin, my friend. That was him then. Both of us young and full of life.

I tipped the dregs from my quart pot onto the dying fire and rolled a fresh cigarette. Daniel watched me. He said, I was never a smoker. I had guessed that. I never yet felt easy with a man who did not enjoy a smoke. We stayed a while then packed up and headed back to the house to catch the horses. The day was well advanced. We was quiet with each other on the way back, Daniel easier in himself. He did not point out nothing to me, that is how I knew his feelings.

FIVE

Daniel parked the jeep in the shed and he went over to the back door with the tucker box. I took our bridles down to the paddock and caught the horses. I do not know what Esme and Daniel had to say to each other. He come out of the house before I had the saddle on Mother. I did not see Esme come to the door to watch us leave and Tip did not bark. I had saddled Daniel's gelding first and it stood there droopy-eyed and trying to catch a quick nap before heading into the day's work. I did not know why a man would keep a horse with such an attitude to a day's work but it was not my business to say. Daniel bought that horse for the police off Ron Parker out at Beelah and Ron was well known for getting rid of things he did not wish to keep. Finisher, Ron Parker called that horse, and it was well named. It was a layabout and had them sleepy eyes. What my dad called a Sunday horse. It would not walk nice and companionable alongside another horse when you was travelling through the bush but was always trying to follow behind, dreaming along, its head down and not watching where it was stepping, tripping on roots and loose stones rolling under its feet, and giving that little cough horses give when they are not happy. It was of a mild temperament and did not have a mean streak at any level but it leaned its weight on me when I shod it. Daniel give it to Irie to learn to ride on. He said it was safe. I told her it was not good to learn to ride on such a horse as she would learn nothing but kicking her heels into its flanks and urging it to stay awake and keep moving. I give her Mother to canter around on, which she did, bareback till Daniel bought her a saddle. I knew Mother would bring that girl home safe. Irie was the only other person I ever let ride Mother. I was proud to see her on Mother's back. Them two took to each other. That thing of Daniel's would have left her and come home alone, stepping on its loose reins and just thinking about itself and its next feed of lucerne hay. Irie knew without me saying nothing to her I would never let anyone ride Mother but her and she blushed when I set her on that mare's back for the first time. Till then I did not know a child could blush. It moved my heart to see it.

. . .

I led off down the bank into the flood of Coal Creek and out across that wide reach of stones where she flattens out and the water is spread over a wide area. There was the taint of our morning's fire in the air. The water come up to our horses' bellies, the stones rattling and clinking under the rush of it, like someone was chipping at a prison wall down there to make their escape. I never did like them loose stones. I was watching upstream in case one of them floating logs come by and was keeping a lookout for a place on the far bank where the horses could get a purchase with their feet. I did not know what the great hurry was to be out there at Ben's place. By the next morning the water would have gone down a couple of foot or more and we could have waited till then. But Daniel was set on it and I seen that. Esme not coming to the door when we was leaving the second time was her telling him nothing had changed since the morning when we left the first time. I believe that was her sign the pressure was still on him to get the thing done. She was a mother and I would say she had strong feelings about Ben's girl. But it was not only that in my opinion but was her way of stiffening Daniel to his policing.

The far bank was all crumpled and broken away by the water, big chunks of grassy clods tipped in and washing out. The bank was nothing but silt, ten foot of it, straight up mostly, with a lip at the top where the grass roots was holding the silt together. I seen a place where a dead tree had broken down the lip and I guided Mother downstream a little way to get her next to it. I was going very easy as I did not want Mother stepping into a hole. She was snorting and reaching her neck and was not happy to be urged into this, but I knew her to be reliable and willing and she had never come down with me yet. My boots filled up with water. It was cold. We come out of the water and lunged up into the breakaway, the silt bank giving under the thrusting of her hind legs. She was lurching and foundering and I was ready to step off when she found a purchase and got herself up onto the bank with a great heave and a grunt. She stood on the bank and shook herself, nearly shaking me off. I looked around and seen Daniel struggling up the breakaway on Mother's tracks. He was out of the saddle and up over the neck of that old gelding of his, its eye white and frantic. The pair of them looked like they was going over backwards into the water any minute. Finisher went down on his knees and Daniel had his boots dragging in the silt. They ended up back in the creek again, side-on to the bank. Daniel reefed the Finisher around on the rein and swore at him, sticking his spurs into that soft hide, the red stain of the blood sluicing away with the water.

I was getting no pleasure at all watching the performance. I turned away and seen Ben's place over on my right-hand side on that piece of high ground where he set it, maybe a hundred and fifty yards off through the timber. A little less than that. His old International truck inside the shed. I seen its red roof flickering through the thin leaves. I sat looking over the horses in the paddock beyond Ben's stockyards. The old packhorse, Lazy, was not there and nor was Ben's young entire that he called Muscles. Ben always liked to ride a stallion. Muscles was an iron-footed tough little pony that he bred his stock from. There was four mares looking over towards me from the other side of the fence, a new foal with one of them and two others heavy in foal. The black and white pony he called Stumbles was not there neither.

Daniel come up beside me. I looked at him and I said, They are gone off for stores more than likely. Them big storms has been keeping Fay off the road with that Blitz of hers. Ben and his girl will have gone to the Dawsons' place to stock up.

Daniel stepped down and led out to the end of his reins, Finisher planting his feet and not moving off with him. Daniel stood at the full stretch of the reins, Finisher's jaw sticking out and his eyes wide. Daniel unbuttoned his flies and had a long pee. When he was done he turned around and eased back on the reins. How do you know that? he said. I set Mother into a walk. Well, I know it,

I said. You will see how it is. Daniel did not climb back on board Finisher but led him along behind me. He did not say nothing more just then. I stepped down at the rails and Daniel come up to me. His clothes was all wet. So do you think Rosie was mistaken? he said. I said, Rosie sees things we do not see. Daniel said nothing to this. I looped Mother's reins through themselves and pushed her off just like I was pushing a boat off from the shore to float with the current, gently easing her flank aside. I ran my hand down her rump as she turned away and walked off towards the green pick the other side of the clearing. I was smiling with the pleasure of it. Mother was the best mare I ever had. I seen Daniel was about to set Finisher loose in the same manner and I knew I had to say something to him or he would be walking home. I would hitch that horse to the rails, I said, or he will decide he is finished for the day and will go home and leave you here to make your way home the best way you can. Daniel looked at his horse and he laughed and patted it on the neck. So that is why they call you Finisher, he said. Finisher give him that queer back-eyed look a horse will give you when it is thinking of nipping you for some offence.

Daniel looped the reins over the rails then turned around and looked at me. I was rolling a cigarette. So does that mean you believe Rosie more than you would otherwise? I licked the paper and closed the cigarette off and nipped off the threads that always poke out the ends. More than I would otherwise what? I said. Daniel said, More than you would if Rosie did not see things that we do not see. I lit the cigarette and took it from between my lips and inspected it. I said, If Rosie Gnapun did not see things we do not see she would not be Rosie Gnapun but would be some other woman. I had had enough of the conversation and I walked over to Ben's dwelling.

Me and Ben built the place out of sheets of ripple iron we salvaged from the picture theatre in Mount Hay after it was burned down by that bunch of stockmen who come in from Mount English that time and went wild when there was nothing left to drink at Chiller's. Them sheets of iron was all twisted up and rusted when me and Ben got them but we hammered them out and they did the job. We loaded them sheets onto the tray body of Ben's International and tied them down with our broncoing ropes. We cut bush poles for the framing of the shed, which is what it was, and wired them together with number eight fencing wire. It was not a place you could call a house with any truth but was one open space inside without no divides. Ben did not like divides anyhow. He liked to see what was around him. A zinc tub hung out the side by the galley where Ben kept his tools. Bars and axes and shovels and one or two other things he kept there, a wheelbarrow upended against the wall. The tub was not for bathing but was for when we was cleaning a sucking pig we had shot. Ben liked to clean the guts and fry them. His grandfather taught them to eat pigs' guts, but I never could come at them, not after the stink of cleaning them. Ben was a number one munga man and was known to eat anything was put in front of him. And there was the creek for bathing and washing clothes. It was a good place to settle on. In the driest time that big hole directly down the bank was always full. I never seen her with less than five or six feet of water in her at the driest. And always clear, except when the creek was up with the storms as it was now. There must have been a spring come out from under them rocks. That is why Ben set his place there. It was like him. There was any amount of jewfish and black bream in that hole. Both good eating.

Like I said, I helped Ben put her up. It took the two of us one week from go to whoa. The side windows, which was hinged flaps of iron on timber frames, was down that day owing to the storms. I seen the door was blown open from the wind and there was a puddle of rainwater with yellow leaves floating in the hollow where you step in at the door. Them yellow leaves was off the bauhinia tree out the front that I did not mention before. I went inside and saw Ben's old single-shot .22 rifle that he kept handy by the door. It was knocked over and lying on the floor. I picked it up and rubbed the dirt off the barrel and set it against the lintel of the door where it was kept. Coal Creek was snake country and Ben would shoot any snake that come around the place except a carpet snake. A big old carpet snake camped with him for a season. He said it kept the mice and rats down. Ben called it Sweetheart. He never fed it nothing to keep it hungry. I asked him how he knew the snake was a girl, and he said, A sweetheart don't have to be a girl, Bobby. Ben always had an answer for you. That snake spent its days sleeping curled in a heap in that dark corner behind where Ben kept his gear. I never seen it eat a mouse or a rat or even move. I used to wonder to myself if it had dreams. I never seen an animal that liked to sleep so much as that snake did. It must have known it had a friend in Ben or it would not have stayed around. I do not remember it ever dying, but I do know it was no longer there. Ben never said when it left. Even a snake as sleepy as that one must have to go off and mate with another snake sometime, or the whole race of snakes would die out from sleep and pure laziness.

It was half dark inside and I stepped across and pushed up the first window flap and set the pole against the stop, letting daylight in. I stood looking out the window towards the creek. The afternoon was well on and the sun was behind us and hanging low over Mount Dennison. The long shadows of the bauhinia spraying all across the green pick and lighting up Mother's coat, which looked the colour of a fox just for a minute there, except Mother's coat was glossy with them oats I was feeding her and foxes I have seen have not been glossy. I turned around from the window as Daniel come to the door. I said to him, I do not think Ben would wish me to invite you inside his place, boss. It was unusual for me to call Daniel boss but I did not feel good with what I was saying and wished to offer him a sign to make it easier for him.

Daniel stopped where he was, not in nor outside, his boots in the puddle. I kept my eyes on him, although I would have rather looked at something else. He stared back at me, his look steady and with some surprise and maybe with something of contempt in it. It was plain he had not been expecting this from me and did not like to hear it. Well that's too bad, he said. I believe I have the authority to enter Tobin's place as I am here on police business. As you are yourself, Bobby. I hope you are not going to forget that.

It was the first time I ever heard his tone hardened up, like he was warning me. I did not wish to be tested by Daniel on this but I seen he was determined to put me to it now it had come to it. Well, I said, speaking as easy as I could but my throat was tight with it and my voice come out unnatural, I believe Ben would dispute that authority of yours if he was here.

I did not wish to say this but I knew I was going to regret not saying it when Ben come home, as he was sure to ask me if the constable had been looking through his place. I have found it is no good failing the truth of something when the test of it comes to you. It might feel easy to lie but sooner or later you are always found out. If I did not speak out now I knew my chance to do so later would be gone. But all the same I did not feel good about doing it.

Daniel laughed like he was saying he did not care one way or the other for Ben's ideas of his authority. Well, Bobby, he said, Rosie was right about them two not being here. And it seems to me she may well be right about the rest of her claims too, and you may be the one who is mistaken in this. We'll be running out of daylight soon and we should be riding out in search of them if we are to pick up their tracks before dark and get some idea of their direction.

I took the cigarette from my lips and looked at it. I did not think there was a need to be riding anywhere. I said, You don't see no signs of violence here and neither do I. Them two ponies has been ridden off the place in good order and no one in a hurry to get away. Anyone who knows Ben's stock can see they took old Lazy to bring home their supplies on from the Dawsons' place. They will be home here in the morning, the two of them. I would lay my life on that.

Daniel did not come on any further into the house but stood where he was and I seen I had set him thinking. I turned around and walked down the length of the place to opposite where the bunks was and I opened the side door and went out. You cannot see the creek from the side door of Ben's place but I could hear the roar of it going over the rocks. The galley where Ben done his cooking was over to my left. The iron roof we put over it was leaning to one side. It would be needing new poles and I thought I would come out and help Ben set them in. If I was out of the police I would have time and a good state of mind to do some work with him again. It would be easier for me to get away from Daniel and Esme and the police house for a while. The only thing with not being at the police house was I would be leaving Irie behind and risking losing my friendship with her. It was Irie was keeping me in the police with Daniel. I stood smoking my cigarette and listening to the roar of the creek and thinking about myself and how I was going to behave. I did not wish to lose Irie's friendship. That was number one with me now. My mother understood me closely on this. My mother and Irie would have liked each other and been friends. In my thinking on all this I could not get past the fact that my friendship with Irie Collins was just about the most precious thing in my life just then. I was held in a bond by it, and I seen there was a price on that bond if I was to keep it. But I did not at that time see the whole price. That come later.

And when it come it was steeper than I could ever have imagined it would be. Some might say it was too steep. I do not say that.

I dropped the butt of my cigarette and stepped on it and went back inside. Through the door at the end, out behind Daniel in the last of the sunlight, I seen Finisher walking off towards where Mother was grazing, trailing his reins and stepping on them, snapping his head up. I said, He's come loose. Daniel turned around and he cursed and went after him, calling to him to hold up. When Finisher seen Daniel coming after him he threw up his head and broke into a trot. Which is what I would expect him to do. Daniel might have offered that horse a scoop of oats but he chased him instead. I had told Daniel to hitch him to the rail and Daniel had not taken care to do that but had just tossed the reins over the rail and left it at that. Daniel called out to Finisher and that horse lifted himself and looked back over his shoulder and stepped higher, smelling his freedom and the comforts of the home paddock. Mother stopped feeding and looked over at him. She watched him a moment then ducked her head and went back to grazing the sweet grass. I did not feel inclined to disturb Mother and go after Daniel's horse for him, which would be an insult to most men I knew to catch their horse for them. I watched Daniel going after that horse and I wondered if it was not too late to hope for much from him.

I sat on the bench Ben had made to go down one side of his long table. The timbers was from a crow's ash pine, and was split and adzed by him, worn dark and shiny now with being used. Crow's ash is not an easy timber to work. I run the flat of my hand over the top of the table and I thought maybe I should resign from the police right now and be done with it, say the word as soon as Daniel come back with Finisher. Being in on this business with him against Ben was dark in me and I knew I could not shake it. I always knew there was something not right about going into the police, which I had done really out of interest to be doing something different from mustering the scrubs. I had not seen the whole thing was not right, and not just me being out here hunting my friend with the Mount Hay constable, which was something I had not seen coming. But that was what my situation was and I could not lie to myself about it.

My thoughts on all this was distracted by something yellowish lying underneath the rail across from me where Ben kept his spare saddles and gear. I got up off the bench and went around the table and looked at what it was. It was a piece of pinewood shaped into the head of a horse. I picked it up and held it off and turned it around to see it in the light. It had the look of a horse head all right, but small, the wood grain showing close and yellow, fragrant with the seeping oils. I put it to my nose and closed my eyes and took in the smell. There was a good many dark knots which I could see Ben had taken time to dig around and shape with the knife. Which would not have been easy for anyone to do. The cypress pine is a wood that will split and crack open but this piece was sound. I had seen the needles of the pine used as a smoking medicine by Rosie's people, the sick person standing in the smoke and sweating out the sickness of their mind or their body. You do not see many of them trees this far into the ranges, but when you do see them they usually stand together like a small family knowing itself out of place. There was chips and shavings and pieces of the yellow wood laying about on the floor. I set the carved horse head down in its place again and went back and sat at the table where I was sitting when I seen it. I had never known Ben to carve nothing and I had difficulty seeing him doing it. But I knew when Ben decided to do something he was sure to make a fine job of it. Ben did not go on with a thing unless he was getting it right.

I was puzzling on these thoughts and the whole situation and looking across at Ben's spare saddles sitting on the rail opposite me, along with his bridles and hackamores and a couple of hard-twist cotton rope surcingles he was restringing, and I was thinking about that life I had known well with him and how it was now in the past for me though I was still a young man and not yet twenty-one.

There was plaited whips and a length of greenhide broncoing rope, and two of them bull straps with the quick-release buckles hanging over saddle cloths. A couple of old leather jackets and Ben's best hat on a peg which Ben only wore when he come into Mount Hay to do some drinking. His dad's spurs was hanging on a high peg above the good hat. All that stuff hanging there looked like Ben himself. I could see him in it. I could smell him. It made me smile thinking of him.

Him and his dad always rode in them military saddles with the kidney boards to save the scalding we sometimes got on horses with tender backs. I never seen a scald on a horse's back from a military saddle. I never did use one of them myself but always rode in a straight-out stock saddle like my own dad. I still had my dad's saddle over at my quarters at the police house. I had his spurs and his hat and his bridles too. I kept all them things of Dad's after he passed away. Seeing Ben's gear hanging there made me think of the time in the future when Ben was to be passed away himself. I seen Ben's place in my eye when we was all done and gone, me and him and Daniel and his interfering wife Esme, who I liked anyway, and that fine mare of mine. This place just being eat up by white ants, pieces of rusting iron all to show for it and for our passing by this way and the joy we had had in our lives, and our troubles too. I had witnessed such places often out there in the scrubs. Desolate, they always was. The hopes of people gone to nothing and forgotten. No names to remember them by. Like the poor who lie in their graves, without no carved and fancy headstones. No one knowing who had dwelled there for their brief time, but only knowing someone had been by there and put their hands to work. I had sat my horse with my dad and looked on such scenes many times and we had smoked a cigarette and paused before moving on with our own business, which was usually getting them half-wild cattle out of the scrubs for some station owner. It was the voice of my mother telling me I should resign from working for the police, I knew that. But I was resisting listening to her on account of fearing to lose Irie and the hope for both of us in the future. I had come to value this hope very highly. More highly than I should have, perhaps. If it had not been for Irie and my secret hopes for our future I would not have hesitated that day but would have told Daniel I could not go on with this thing and must leave the police and be my own man again as working for him did not suit me. Which was only true. But I did not follow the truth of my feelings on that.

Sitting there on the bench at Ben's table I knew myself to be on the cross, part of me going one way and the other part going the other way. I wanted the selfish part of me to win and I did not want it to win. It was a divided feeling, one side fighting with the other side. So I decided to make my decision when Daniel returned from chasing his horse. If I ever seen him again and he did not get lost in the scrub and become bones himself out there in the bendee, the rattlepod growing up out of his eye sockets like that old bull, making a mockery of his dreams of finding his home in the ranges.

The secret hope I cherished to myself but did not voice to anyone, not even in my thoughts to my own mother, had grown in me and I wished to hold it to myself as long as I could hold it. It was the one thing that was my own and belonged to no one else. But it was not in my power to be the boss of it. It was selfish to desire it, but I desired it all the same. One day Irie was going to come into her womanhood and I hoped we was still around each other when that day come. It was not a hope that had much in it, I am willing to admit that, but I could not help holding to it and dreaming it when I was alone and had the chance to think on such things. I imagined conversations with Irie in the future when she was a grown-up girl, which in some ways I had seen she already nearly was. Sometimes I seen the grown woman in Irie's eyes, especially when she was looking serious and defying her mother. Irie was not like Esme and could have been the daughter of some other woman. Miriam was more like her mother and Esme favoured that younger girl. You could see it in her touch. But

Miriam was jealous of Irie's liking for me. Me and Miriam was not friends and we never would be. I knew that and I did not try to be friends with her. She seen the world in different colours to Irie's way of seeing it. Irie seen the world in the same colours I seen it. We had no need to speak of this but knew it to be so between us. We could smile and mean things neither she nor I wished to speak of, but a feeling that was fine and good passed between us on those occasions. Things that was not words but was better than words lay between me and Irie. Words is not good for much when it comes to them feelings.

I was making myself unhappy thinking these thoughts as I knew there was little hope of them ever becoming my real life. I seen something useful I could be doing and I got off the bench and went back out the side door and I took a shovel and the wheelbarrow over to the pile of ant nest and I dug in till I hit the dry stuff and filled the barrow with it. When the barrow was full I pushed it around to the front door and filled the puddle with the ant nest till the water rose up around the sides of it and the ant nest was sitting proud of the floor. The entire floor was tamped ant nest that we had crushed out. I dug a channel to drain off the water and tamped the patch down hard with the back of the shovel. It felt good whacking at it with the back of the shovel, the thumping going out around me in the quiet of that still afternoon, the sound of the creek and the cry of birds giving to that place its own silence, which I loved to be in. I soon forgot to be unhappy. I stood up to ease my back and I seen one of them black falcons sitting in the bauhinia watching me like he was thinking of going home to tell his people a story about me whacking the earth. I told him I had seen him and I stood back to admire what I had done and I asked him if he thought it was okay. That falcon flew and Mother give a low whinny. I turned around and seen Daniel riding Finisher into the clearing. He was kicking that horse along and looking pleased with himself.

I took the barrow and the shovel around to the galley and put them back where Ben kept them. When I come back to the front Daniel had stepped down off Finisher and was standing holding the reins. He was looking off in the direction he just come from. His shirt was dried off but his moleskins still looked heavy with creek water. He did not look at me but just said, like he had made a discovery, I saw their tracks crossing a patch of open ground going out that way. He lifted his hand and indicated, just like Dad used to. Which was the first time I ever seen him do that. He turned and looked at me and he said, We had better head on out there after them, or we will be travelling in the dark.

I had thought of what I would say to him about leaving the police but I did not say it. After the silence had gone on awhile and he was staring at me, he said, I have the feeling I can't be sure you will be with me against Ben Tobin if we should come to a hard situation with him.

I did not know what to say to this, mainly because I did not know the answer to it myself. I did not wish to lie to Daniel, nor even to half lie, which in my opinion is twice as bad as lying straight out. So I said nothing about it and instead I said to him, It seems to me if you was to ride back to the police house and telephone to them Dawsons they will tell you they have seen Ben and his girl. Then you will not need to take my word for these things and you will be satisfied with the word of Frank Dawson, or his wife Anne, if it is her you speak to and Frank is out in the country as he most often is. I might have left it at that but I went on, And then Mrs Collins will stop pressing you to some action where you are not sure of the outcome. I was pushing things saying this, I knew that. But I felt things needed pushing or I was going to be in trouble with both sides of this.

Daniel did not say nothing in reply but kept looking at me, his eyes narrowed somewhat and his mouth working as if he intended to spit, but he did not. I never seen Daniel spit. I said, The Dawsons will tell you they seen Ben and his girl. I know that. Daniel turned away from me and he looked at Finisher as if he was going to say something to the horse, and he said in a quiet voice, You are very sure of yourself, Bobby, about this. Yes, I said, I am sure of myself about this. I will stay here and wait for Ben and his girl and I will ride back to the police house in the morning and give you my report. Daniel thought a while, reaching and rubbing Finisher's nose, which that horse did not mind, as it made him think he might be going to get something to eat. Daniel did not turn around and look at me, and when he spoke again his voice was low and quiet and thinking. And what if the Dawsons have not seen Ben Tobin and his girl? Now he did turn around and look at me. What then, Bobby? What do you suggest I do then? He was looking at me in a way like he thought I would not have an answer for him to this question.

I said, Ben will be back here at first light with his stores. There is nothing here for them two to eat. I have looked. There is no flour in that bin and no tinned meat and their fruit tins is finished except for them pineapple chunks. Which I know are not Ben's favourites. He would have ordered them only when Fay told him there was nothing else to get from the Mount Hay store. I know that. This is where Ben lives. His things is all here. And anyway, we cannot go chasing off after them tracks in this light. Once you are in the scrub it is not so easy to see. The night comes down early in the scrub and stays late. If something has been done to that girl that should not have been done to her we are not going to undo it by chasing off into the scrub at this hour.

Daniel give some thought to what I said. He sniffed a couple of times, drawing in his breath, and he looked down and plucked at his moleskins where they was clinging to his thighs. I did not know how he was going but I was hungry. His moleskins was still heavy with creek water. He said, As you know so much about our Mr Ben Tobin, I will do this your way. He looked at me straight. I said, I am sure you will not regret it. Mrs Collins will be glad to see you tonight and gladder still when you have spoken to the Dawsons and set her mind at rest, which you can easily do over the telephone as soon as you gets in. Daniel said, We shall see. He turned around and gathered the reins and put his foot in the stirrup and got up on board Finisher.

He sat looking down at me the way people will look down at you from a horse when they are talking to you and you are on foot, his boots pointing their toes at me out of the stirrups like them boots knew who I was. That Webley revolver looked big and heavy on his belt. I seen his hand go to it, his fingers fumbling at the buckle and him taking it out and aiming it at my head. Looking into the barrel of a gun pointed at me, that round hole staring at me like a blind eye, black and hollow with no feelings in it for me. I was in a kind of daze imagining this happening to me, Daniel deciding in his mistrust that he must get rid of me altogether. In my daze I knew if I was shot by him at this moment I would disappear and not be just any ordinary dead body lying there but would not be there at all. Not anywhere. No sign of me, and as if I had never been. I seen him grin and put that gun away again, looking real satisfied with himself, like he had proved himself the better man.

I come out of my daze when he said, Well, Bobby, you will get nothing for your dinner tonight. And he grinned at me, like he knew he had really shot me and it was his secret that I could not know and was dead. I said, That is true, but I have gone without my dinner other times and it has not killed me. He said, I can expect to see you back at the police house in the morning then? I said, That is for sure. I seen he still had his doubts and was a long way from being entirely satisfied to put his trust in me. I wondered suddenly if he thought maybe me and Ben was together in some kind of a plot against him. I had not had such a thought before, but once it come to me I found myself watching for signs of it. That perhaps he was testing me. There was something else he had to say before he left. You said Rosie sees things we do not see, he said. Now you are asking me to believe that we do not see those things because they are not really there. If Rosie is right and you are wrong, then we are giving Ben Tobin a twenty-four-hour start on us and I am failing to act on Rosie Gnapun's report of murder. He did not wait for me to say nothing to this but left it with me to think on and swung away and set Finisher into a trot and headed across the clearing, sitting askew in that big saddle of his the way he did, as if he was half ready to step off. The way he rode set a horse off-balance and I did not like to see it.

I stood watching him riding into the evening light, going down towards that crumbly silt bank where we had made our crossing. I seen him go down over the bank and I looked at the sky. Them high curved clouds was all gone and the sky was clear, purpling at the horizon. The sun was gone off the flat too and was golden among the top branches of the brigalow, a chill beginning in the air. Daniel had turned around and raised his hand as he was going over the bank, and I wondered if he had had some second thought about me and how we stood. He would not be back at the police house before dark. I believed there was a fair chance of him missing his way and getting confused in the bendee. I did not think he was convinced by what I had said to him. I was not convinced of it myself. I wished I could have been more straight with him but I did not see how that might be done without speaking to him of my secret hopes of Irie and my pleasure in the friendship of that child. Which was something I knew I could not do. All them thoughts belonged in my own head and nowhere else. A stick of gelignite blowing everything to pieces if they ever did come out of my head into the open, Esme and Daniel looking at me like I was a devil come to destroy their child and their happiness. I knew all right where them thoughts of mine about Irie belonged and where they would land me if I ever did let them out. I knew that clear and clean as I knew my own mother's name. My mother's name was Mary. The nuns give it to her. She did not know the name her own mother give to her. She liked being Mary and it suited her.

The fear I had was that Daniel was getting disappointed in his adventure in the ranges and was losing the dream he had of it for his family when he brought them up from the coast after the war had been keeping them all apart for them anxious years. I was afraid he would be making a decision to return his family to the coast soon enough. Which was where they rightly belonged. And nothing was clearer to me than that. Daniel was never going to be at home up in that wild old scrub country of ours. He might hold to it if Esme made him do it but he would not belong. I could not see that such a man for good order and neatness was ever going to fit with the way things was done in Mount Hay. I did not know why our town was called Mount Hay. There was no mountain and there was no hay thereabouts. Esme was another story to Daniel. I seen she was the kind of person to push hard at what she wanted, and not be content till she got it all facing the way she wanted it facing. I had a blue dog like that once. Some old scrubber bull would get his backside in a thorn bush and face that dog down head-on. But that dog never give up till he got the bull to rush him. Then he was behind that old bull and swinging from its tail. I had that dog from a pup and called him Smiley because he always looked like he was smiling at me. He was trod by a heifer in the yards out at Beelah and had his back broke and my dad had to shoot him. I was not able to do it myself. I never had a dog after Smiley. My dad did not like working with dogs. That was Esme. Always smiling and persisting. A blue cattle dog. I believe she could have made her home anywhere, Mount Hay or anywhere else if she had a mind to do it. She would just keep at it till she had things lined up her way. If the place did not suit her she would make it suit her. Daniel was not going to resist her when she was pushing but was inclined to quit the whole thing and go her way. Which was what he had just done with me, going my way with this hunt for Ben, unless it was all just a test of me. All the same I do not believe Esme would have resisted Daniel if he had come back to the police house at the end of a day and told her point blank, We are leaving this place and going home. I think there would be no arguing with Daniel once he was pushed to the point where he decided to stick on something big like that.

SIX

On my own out there at Coal Creek that evening I stood outside Ben's place after Daniel was gone down over the bank and I watched the night coming on around the edge of the scrub. I liked the quiet and my solitude. The cry of birds overhead going home for the night to wherever they go, driving through the evening sky with confidence, calling to each other, flocks of them crying at the end of the day like they was lamenting the end of life itself. I looked up and watched them going over and I asked myself, Do birds know the sun will rise again in the morning, or do they think the darkness is come down forever? And I did not know the answer. How can we know what birds think? If they only wanted water there was plenty of water for them right there in Coal Creek. I do not like to hear a man claim that animals and birds do not think. The man who says that is not thinking himself but is just blowing himself up to look bigger than things he has no understanding of. You would never hear a blackfeller saying animals and birds do not think. They know better. It was not water them birds was looking for but some big stand of old wild fig trees. There is not many of them fig trees in the ranges, but I knew such a tree. A thousand years old my dad said it was. And maybe older than that by far. Who could tell the true age of such a tree? That great old tree grew beside a pure spring deep in the scrubs up against the ironstone flank of Mount Coats, its many trunks and roots growed into the crevices and across the planes of the stone, and the stone and the wood of the tree was wedded to each other like the tree had become molten. The air was always cool and sweet under the great canopy of that tree, the water of the spring deep and clear, blades of sunlight striking through the water to the stones on the bottom, an old-man eel six foot long living in the mouth of the spring. The spirit of that spring I would call him. And how old was he? A thousand years old too? Old, for sure.

Me and my dad and Ben and his dad camped there when we was chasing them scrubber bulls over in that lonely country. We always stayed there longer than we had a need to. It was such a fine place to be. Ben's grandfather had known it. That fig tree spring, as we called it, come into my dreams often since Dad passed on and I believe that is where his spirit went. The spread of that old tree was a hundred yards in every direction except up against the stone face of the mountain, them pale roots all glossy and hanging down from the high spread of the branches like they was hanging from the ceiling of a church, coming down in the soft light through the leaves, fat and green, the branches heavy with them little purple fruits, all speckled and sweet to the taste of the possums and the flying foxes which was always there when the fruit come ripe. When the fig tree spring come into my dreams my mother was always out there with us. Nothing was said in my dreams between her and my dad but in the dream I knew they was happy to be there with me and with each other. It was my happiness dream. I always felt good after having it.

I told Irie about that place and my feelings for it and she took my hand in hers and made me swear a solemn oath to her that I would take her there one day, which I was fool enough to swear to. I do not know how any person could have resisted her, sitting there gripping my hand in her own warm hands and looking with that great innocent seriousness of hers into my eyes, as if she thought I was the most special person she had ever met or ever would meet, and she could place her trust in me and be at ease with me. I took that oath with Irie though I knew it was most unlikely I would be able to keep to the terms of it. Which is the way things are for us and our dreams mostly, so it seems to me, in this life. But I do not know why that should be. They just is and that is all there is to be said of it.

Standing out there beside Ben's galley on my own with the evening to myself and my dreams of what life might yet hold for me if only things could go my way, I knew how glad I was to be rid of Daniel . . . A great fire like the fire of the last days was raging across the scrubs before my eyes, red and orange flames devouring all that stood in their path, the roaring and the howling of the fire wind, and I was running fast as a wild horse towards the police house, the flames licking and wrapping around them boards, the tin curling from the roof, and I was inside and Irie seen me and I picked her up and carried her outside and I was so strong I outran the fire and flew over the scrub with her till we was at the fig tree spring, her entire family lost and the town burned down like the old picture theatre and only Irie and me left to care for each other. I shivered to think of the beauty of it.

I was getting a chill through my shirt standing there, so I walked over and untied my jacket from the back of my saddle and put it on. I could still see them flames. My imagination of such a fire frightened me it was so real. I could feel it in me and I feared it, for I did not know how to stop such a raging thing if it come up from inside me. When you go in a daze you do not know what is a vision and what is real to touch with your hand. I spoke to Mother and she followed me over to the small yard and I unsaddled her and let her loose. Ben's mares come up to the rails and looked in at her, tossing their heads and kicking up and showing off as horses will in front of a stranger. They are no different to us in that way. I carried my gear back to the house and took Mother a scoop of oats out of the bin Ben had there with a wooden lid on it to keep the rats out that Sweetheart had not killed off. If that old snake had died and had not drifted off somewhere looking for a mate it would have been the rats that ate her corpse. I thought of that. The rats eating the snake that ate their own parents. It was like the rats was eating themselves. There was a half forty-four-gallon drum filled with sweet water in the small yard for her. I stood back and watched Mother lipping them oats and when I had seen enough I went around to the galley and lit myself a fire. I made a drink of tea and rolled a cigarette.

I thought I might eat one of them cans of pineapple chunks later on. Or maybe two. They was not my favourites neither and I would have liked a can of corned beef and some fresh bread and potatoes, but I had seen there was nothing to be had, only that pile of empty cans out the back attracting the rats, them horse thistles growing up through the pile with all the rain they had been having out there. While I was watching the billy coming to the boil I was remembering Esme telling Daniel he was all that stood between the young women—which was her words—and the likes of brutal men such as Ben. And it seemed to me the evil of her misunderstanding was working itself into things and was in that opinion of Esme's and her putting it on Daniel that he become some kind of protector of young women. I knew Esme would not have taken my word against Rosie's. I knew that. Not ever. No matter what I said. That day Rosie come by and Esme come out of the house and lifted her up and took her in her arms Esme had decided she and Rosie was some kind of sisters. But I do not think Rosie had decided Esme Collins was her sister. Rosie had her own sisters, and she had her own thoughts. Which was too deep for Esme Collins.

The water come to the boil and I tossed in some tea and lifted the billy off the fire with a piece of bent iron rod Ben kept there for that purpose. That rod was a gearstick from an old Willys Overland. There was no one else like Irie had ever been in my life out there at Mount Hay nor in the scrubs with my dad all them years. Being invited to eat with her family was a kindness of Esme's, but I knew I was not family and never would be fit to think of Irie as I did think of her. Not in the eyes of Esme and Daniel Collins. And I did not know how I might keep her with me if they was to leave the town. I carried the billy inside and I sat at the table and poured tea into a tin mug and I drank from the mug. There was a bitterness in the tea that made my teeth squeak. Ben must have mixed in some ground-up cumby cumby leaves with the tea for his stomach pains. I wished he had not done that.

SEVEN

I brought my right hand slowly out from under the blanket and reached to touch the thing that was hovering close to my left eye. There was a small tremble in the thing. As my hand got close to the thing it drew back. So I drew my hand back. The thing moved down again to an inch off my eye so that it was fuzzy. I did not know what it was and I wondered if I was having one of my dazes. But I knew I was not. My sight come clear and I seen she was standing over me, one foot each side of me at around my waist. She was sighting down Ben's .22 that he kept by the door, the point of the barrel near touching my eyeball. I could see her finger curled around the trigger. I knew that gun to be old and somewhat light-triggered. It had seen a lot of use and had belonged to Ben's grandfather. I could feel the bullet going into my eye and out the back of my skull into my rolled-up jacket that I had put under my head when I lay down. I thought it was a pity to make a hole in that jacket.

Behind her the doorway was a soft grey crossed with a pink streak of early dawn. Looking at the dawn a strange feeling come over me then of drifting, like I was floating a foot above the floor but seeing myself from far off and knowing I was going over into a blessed and caring place where none of my troubles would follow me. I had no fear but a quiet kind of happiness.

Her voice come down to me. Who're you? And I knew she was a Murri by the sound of her. I said, I am Bobby Blue. I did not want this conversation with her but wanted to stay floating and going over into the place of peace and beauty that was waiting for me beyond the dawn—that is how it seemed, beyond the dawn. Them words was in my mind and I liked to hear them. I knew a man might wait a lifetime to hear them words. I had no regret at leaving this life or any of the things in this life, but just a small regret for Irie. And this surprised me, that it was not a bigger regret but was a sound some way off. That I could feel things so differently just because I had the eye of death looking at me. My hopes for Irie belonged to some other place that was not of the new world beyond the dawn. It was not me I felt sorrow for, it was Irie to be left behind. I had no concern for my own sorrows.

Her voice come down to me again. What the hell you smilin at? I got this rifle pointed at your eye and you smilin. You got no reason to smile, boy. You don't look like the Bobby Blue he been telling me about. The point of that rifle just wavering no more than a fraction, like the eye of the barrel was inspecting me for the exact spot.

Well I am him, I said. I am lying down and I do not look as I do when I am standing up, which is how Ben would have described me to you. My horse is out there in the small yard and Ben will know it is me as soon as he sees that mare of mine. The girl shifted her weight and I felt the touch of her spur through my shirt where the blanket was half off me. I said, Your spur is getting into my side. She did not shift her boot away from my side but pressed it in harder. If you move I'll shoot your eye, she said. I said, I am not moving. Why don't you ask Ben? She sniffed. Ben aint here. I said, Well you and me are in a fix then. She said, It is you in the fix, not me. I said, What is your name? She said, That is nothing to you. Ben will be here soon enough. He is following the tracks of that feller who ate the other tin of pineapple chunks you left on the table. I said, I ate both those tins. Is that so? she said, being sarcastic. We crossed them tracks out there in the scrub and Ben seen there is two of you hanging about here and he gone to get that other one. That feller better watch out.

You are Deeds, I said. If I am not Bobby Blue how do I know that? She said, I don't care how you know it. Keep still or you are dead and then you'll know nothin. I did not think she was going to shoot me now, but only by an accident of pressing on that fine trigger a small bit more than she was already pressing on it. The land beyond the dawn was going away fast. I said, I seen you once before.

I heard Ben laughing outside and the stamp and snorting of horses. You had better let me up, I said. Ben come in at the door. He was carrying the bags from the packhorse. He dumped them on the table. You can shoot him now if you want to, Deeds. He laughed some more and come over and looked down at me. What you doing lying down there, Bobby Blue? I suddenly wanted to live again and I valued my life and I knew I loved Irie and would love her forever and I feared that rifle more than I ever feared anything I could think of, that it might go off without that girl Deeds meaning to kill me now that she was paying attention to Ben. I put up my hand and pushed that barrel to one side and I got to my feet. Ben said, This is Deeds. Me and Deeds are going to have a baby, Bobby. If it's a boy we're going to call him Bobby. You will be Uncle Bobby.

Deeds was tall and thin and was wearing a wide-brimmed bull-shooter hat with no bash and them flared American Lee Rider jeans that people got off the soldiers who had stayed behind. Her shirt was one of them fancy black and white things Hoy's used to sell and her jacket was paired with the jeans. She had one of her front teeth missing. The left one. The gap did no harm to how she looked and it suited her in a way I cannot describe. I do not know where she got the jacket and the jeans from. I would like to have had them myself. She was a pretty smart-looking girl. I had seen her when Ben was getting himself arrested by Daniel that first time. I had probably also seen her in Mount Hay, hanging about giggling with a bunch of other kids out the front of Hoy's store. I would say she was no more than sixteen. If she was that. I am not good with ages and dates and I may be out on that one. She kept hold of the rifle but did not point it at me. She said to Ben, You get that other one? Oh, that old boy's gone, Ben said. With any luck he broke his neck going over that breakaway on the creek bank. I never seen so much scuffing and charging about the place as I seen out there where he was trying to catch his horse. I wish I could have been there to see him tripping over them bendee roots. I said, The constable did not come inside here, Ben. I know that, Ben said. We'll have a feed. I could eat half a bullock. I said, I will eat the other half. Deeds went over and stood the pea rifle by the door in its place. That was a single-shot rifle. A one-chancer is what I always thought of it.

Ben and Deeds was about the same height, only he was a lot thicker in the chest than she was, and not nearly so pretty. She was not so dark as Rosie on account of her father being a whitefeller. I was a good two inches taller than the pair of them, but not so thick in the body as Ben. I was not so thick around as Ben, and I liked being the way I was. No one never called Ben Tobin pretty. You could see he had been knocked about a bit. I was glad to see him. I do not know how I would have been with him if Daniel had still been there. And worse still if Daniel had come inside the place and slept on the floor like I did. I was glad I had kept him out and none of that happened to upset things between me and Ben. Seeing Ben and Deeds together laughing and touching each other I knew things had changed between me and Ben from the way they had been before we quit the scrubs. It was in me to tell them about my feelings for Irie. But I knew I would not speak of it. There was a time I would have spoken out to Ben whatever come into my thoughts. That was one change. There might have been others. I am not saying we had become strangers to each other, I never did lose my love for him, but only that things was different now and I respected that and nothing was said of it.

Ben said, Where's that water you're boiling up, Bobby? I'm dying of thirst waiting for that drink of tea. I went out and got some sticks together and lit a fire in the galley. Ben had a pile of split sandalwood beside the galley and I put some on and watched it spitting and cracking, sending up the best smell there is anywhere this side of that last dawn. Ben come out and put some fresh ribs on the steel plate and he stood and poked at them with that old gear lever and smoked his cigarette. He said, Old Dawson killed a heifer. We stood watching the ribs grilling. He said, That constable of yours not hiding out somewhere round about is he? I said, He is either drowned or bushed or at home with his missus by now.

. . .

When the evening come on we lit the kerosene lamp and Ben got out a half-bottle of rum he had there and we drank and he played on that old Hohner harmonica of his. Ben always liked to play that old mouth organ and sing a few words here and there of the songs. They was always sad songs about cowboys dying or losing their sweethearts or dreaming of their mothers or getting hanged or something like that. I liked to hear them but I never sung them myself. Deeds picked up the horse's head he was carving and showed it to me. Ben said, That is the third one I tried. Deeds didn't like the others and told me to get it right. Deeds is a fussy

girl. It is going to be the head of the little feller's rocking horse.
I said, And suppose the little feller is a girl? In that case, Ben said,
we will still call her Bobby. Bobby is as good a name for a girl as it
is for a boy. I had not thought of that before but I seen there was
truth in it. Ben always had the answer.

Deeds giggled and said, I could have shot you dead as a rabbit,
Bobby Blue. I said, I would not have minded one little bit, Deeds.
Do you know that? She said to Ben, I had the barrel nearly in his
eye and he was smilin at me as if I was ticklin him. Ben left off
his playing long enough to say, That is Bobby Blue, Deeds. You
cannot frighten Bobby Blue with a gun. He winked at me and
went back to playing his Hohner, his eyes nearly closed, his right
hand reaching for the rum bottle. Deeds got up and went around
and sat on his knees and leaned her head on his shoulder, and
he freed his left arm and put it around her and held her to him.
I had never thought to see Ben looking so tender in his mind and
I was pleased to see it, but also I was just a little sad knowing he
was not the old Ben I had known pretty much all my life but was
a man with new concerns. I would say for sure he was the happiest
I ever seen him.

He stopped playing again and said, When you going to get
yourself a family, Bobby? I said, When I am ready. Deeds said,
You got someone in mind? I stood up and went outside and peed

against the trunk of the bauhinia tree and I heard them laughing and the notes of that Hohner went silent.

A quarter moon was up and Mother was looking across at me from the yard. She give a low rumble in her throat and tossed her head. Okay, I said. We're going home right now. There is no need to get impatient. I stood out in the night hearing Ben's harmonica starting up again and getting into the feel of it. I always thought the sound of the harmonica was sweeter when it is heard from a distance away. There is a mystery in it then. I thought of our days and nights together in the scrubs all them years when we was boys and young men. I went back inside again and got my gear and went out and put the saddle on Mother and led her up to the front door. I went inside and Ben said, I see you fixed the hole by the door. I said, It was something to do.

He tried out a couple of notes on the Hohner, then he took it out of his mouth and uncurled his arm from around Deeds and he turned around and grinned at me. He looked handsome in the soft yellow light of the kerosene lamp. Being handsome is in a man's eyes. And being ugly is in his eyes too. Ben could look both. He smiled when he seen me looking at him with the gentleness of my thought. He said, I got a nice little surprise in my bag for that constable of yours. I will give it to him for Christmas. But first I am going to let him sweat a while. You seen him sweating,

Bobby? I did not feel too comfortable with this and wanted to get going. It was the first Ben had said of it. I said, I do not think he is sweating, Ben. I think for him it is over between you two and is settled. Ben said quietly, Is that what you think? I don't think you think that, Bobby. That constable of yours put me in Stuart without no reason and I owe the fool something for that. You don't think I should pay my debts, Bobby Blue? I tell you what, he said, I do not pay false debts, like that Auntie Rosie of Deeds' here.

Deeds cut in and said, You beat her boy Orlando real bad that time and she is only paying you what she owes you by making trouble for you now. Rosie's is not a false debt, she said. It is a real debt. I told you to go and talk to her and tell her you would pay off what you owed and to let her know Orlando can come back home and you will not be a trouble to him. She lost her son through you and she's never going to forget it. You know them Old People. They got to get even too. You know that, Ben Tobin. You'll have trouble from Auntie Rosie so long as she's alive to give you trouble unless you go and see her and square your debt with her. I know for sure she put one of them Old Murri curses on you and it will stay on you till she's done with you. That's what she done.

I was impressed to hear Deeds giving it to Ben straight and I seen the girl had a strong mind and a will to do things the way she saw fit and I began to admire her for that. Ben just smiled and went back to playing his mouth organ, sweet and low and sad. But he listened to what Deeds said, his hand stroking her arm, from the round peak of her shoulder to her elbow and back up again, his eyes half closed. You would not know what he was thinking, whether to square things with Rosie or despise her curse and let her see it was not going to work. Which was the old Ben. I seen him listen and say nothing to interrupt Deeds but play that mouth organ real soft so it sounded like it was coming from a long way off and was a tune for her words only. She stroked his stubbly cheek and kissed him and she said softly, You are a strange man, Ben Tobin. There is no one knows you. She turned to me. Aint that right, Bobby Blue?

When Deeds was done he opened his eyes and he looked at me and said, I had no criminal record before your constable Daniel Collins put me in Stuart, Bobby. Now I have a record and people in Mount Hay think of me as a criminal and would be happy if they never seen me again. That's right, aint it? I said nothing to this, but I remembered Ben did not mind one bit going to Stuart and was now seeing things differently to suit himself. He said, All that is on his side and there is nothing on my side. Me and you been together since we was pups. You ever seen me walk away from it when I was called to something? And he give that evil laugh he had. But I looked at him and smiled, for I heard in the way he laughed it was just to show me he was still the man he had been and had not given in to nothing. I did not believe it. When it was real that laugh was hard and menacing and it said more than if Ben said in words he was going to enjoy giving his enemy a hiding.

I heard that laugh of Ben's plenty of times. I do not know how to write it. Ha-ha-ha, like he was saying it and not laughing it, his eyes going starey and spiky without no sign of amusement in them. It was the opposite of a real laugh. I know when he discovered how to do it. I could not do it myself and I would not try to. It come from the hardness in him that his old man put there when we was boys. The laugh first come out of Ben at the last beating his father give him before he died. I remember it as if it was yesterday. We was railing a big mob of old piker bullocks up at the Dobbin yards. It was getting dark and the rain had set in, which we had not been expecting. We was all wet and tired and hungry and was pushing to get the last yard onto them rail trucks and them old bullocks was wise to us and was giving us a hard time of it. I do not know what Ben done to bring on his father's rage but me and my dad suddenly heard his fierce yelling and we seen he was beating at Ben. Ben's dad was old by then and did not have the strength to knock Ben down. And Ben was already grown into the full strength of a man. Ben was standing in the rain taking the beating, and it was not long before his old man ran out of breath and had a fit of coughing. Ben's dad clung to Ben's shirt, coughing and wheezing and spitting up his lungs like he was done for. Ben stood straight and firm and let the old man struggle, the blood running down Ben's face, his hat knocked off and the rain streaking him with the dirt of the yards, his long hair all matted and stitched to his skin. Ben looked like the devil in that evening light. And he was smiling, his teeth white. Ben never once in his life raised his hand to his dad but took the beatings from him like something in him told him they was what was owed him. Ben's dad was hanging off him coughing and shaking, and he soon went to his knees, his hands clawing at Ben's moleskins. Ben stood there straight and still. I remember he was not looking down at his dad but was looking out over that last yard of wild old bullocks we had brought in from the scrubs and had not trucked yet. Ben did not help his father to rise and he did not step away from him. Then suddenly he give this terrible laugh. His old dad was hunched down on the ground, his hands hanging to Ben's moleskins, and he was weeping, his shoulders shaking with his weakness and his despair at something bigger than the beatings he give his son which he was not able to settle with himself. He died of cancer that year. He was just skin and bone when I seen him the last time, his eyes sunk back in his head and his cheeks showing the shape of the bones clear as anything. He looked scared. When I was a boy I never thought nothing would ever scare Ben's dad. Now I seen he was scared of his own death. The smell of him made me sick. That was not more than five months after the beating in the Dobbin yards.

Me and my dad stood watching it till it was done and I know something in my soul was chilled when that laugh come out of Ben. Ha-ha-ha. It was a laugh that come up out of Ben's and his dad's suffering for each other, father and son that they was. If you had known them as me and my dad knew them all those years you would have known this. That laugh changed Ben. We none of us never said nothing about it. That was it. Ben and his dad. We got them heavy bullocks loaded. That is what we did. And they bellowed and horned into each other up the ramp and they made that rail truck rattle with their anger and their humiliation at being boxed. They knew they was never going to roam in the great scrubs of the ranges no more. It was over for them and you heard it in their bawling. I have heard smart people say animals do not know death. But I have seen cattle pawing the ground and bellowing where the carcass of another beast has lain for years, just the bare patch of ground and the few scattered bones the dingoes have left. Them beasts know death all right and those old pikers smelled it in the air that night of Ben's last beating at the Dobbin railhead yards. It was not that real evil laugh he give now out there at Coal Creek that night with Deeds sitting on his lap and having his child inside her. His eyes stayed soft. I seen that. That is why I smiled at him, like I was telling him his laugh did not convince me as it used to. I said, We will see how things go.

. . .

Being with Ben and Deeds out there at Coal Creek for the day and all through that evening of singing and playing the Hohner and drinking that rum and having our feast of ribs I seen how Ben was going to be a good dad and would never beat his child the way his own dad beat him. I seen him stroke her belly and close his eyes and play that mouth organ. No one can resist love. I knew that myself and I feared I would never know with Irie the happiness he had found with Deeds.

I said, The constable has no cause now to go after you again, Ben. He is done with it. And if you would be done with it there will be no more cause for trouble between you. I was still standing in the doorway ready to get up on Mother and ride back to the police house through the night scrubs, which I liked to do more than anything on my own. Ben held the near-empty rum bottle out to me at the full stretch of his arm and he sung one of them songs he was always singing. I do not remember now which one it was. Something sad and about dying and going home. I never sung them songs myself so I do not have them in my mind. He said,

Drink up, old mate, you got a long ride tonight on that brumby mare of yours. Deeds stroked his neck and kissed him where her fingers was, like she was putting a mark on him.

I reached across and took the bottle and I drank and handed it back. I said, Mother is no brumby and you know it. He held the bottle up to the lamp flame then drank off the last quarter inch and he put the bottle down and he turned and looked at me and smiled. I don't like that police shirt on you, Bobby. It don't suit you. I said, Well that's too bad for you, Ben Tobin. We all laughed and I turned around and went out and got up on Mother and I give a wild yell and cantered off across the clearing to the creek bank through the quarter moon. Mother knew what I was about and she gathered herself and give a great leap into the creek from the top of the bank and I let go another mighty yell. I never knew that mare to refuse. She had the courage and good judgment of ten of them stallions of Ben Tobin's and he knew that. Muscles was just muscles that I could see, hard and tough like Ben but stiff in himself. I seen that stiffness in him and it did not suit me. I liked to get the better of them wild cows by cutting them in ways they did not expect. I could do that on Mother. I could do anything on that mare. I did not like to hear her called a brumby. I give another yell from the other side of the creek so Ben would hear me and know we had done it and had not come unstuck. I felt good leaving him with that. Like I had the last smart word. Which was something that did not happen very often with me and Ben. It was usually him coming out with some smart remark at the last. But I had the better of him that time. I rode on feeling pleased with myself.

. . .

After we come up out of Coal Creek, Mother planted herself on the bank and she spread her legs and give herself such a mighty shake I thought the gear was coming off her. When she was finished shaking she straightened up and tossed her head, rattling the bit and letting me know she was ready to move off. I set her over towards the moonlit skyline of that saddle where the last of Long Ridge comes down off Mount Esson and peters out in a stretch of poison bendee. Mother knew where we was heading and eased into the long striding walk she had, which was the easiest ride I had ever had on any horse. Mother was not a horse to stumble and she could weave her way through the brigalow at a flat-strap gallop when we needed to head some beast, which was usually an old cock-horned cow making her run with the knowledge of what was waiting for her in the yards. Once they had read the story them wild cattle was slippery, but Mother could outpace them and turn the fastest of them. I do not wish to exaggerate the ability of that horse, but I cannot help myself paying a tribute to her in this account whenever I see the chance to do it. I knocked back a lot of offers for her and that will tell you it was not just my opinion of her. They used to ask me, Why don't you get a foal out of her while she is still young? But I did not like the idea of being without her for twelve months. There was a sweet little pure-blood Arab out at the Dawsons' place and there was a time when I did think about putting her to him, but I never done nothing about it. Now it is too late for those thoughts. Mother went the same way I was going. We had each other and that was enough for me for the time I had her. I did not like to think of her over there at the Dawsons' place and me riding some other plug. Mother was my friend as well as my horse. Breeding from her was not my idea. I do not think the life she had was poorer for it.

The scrub never looks so pretty as it does with the moonlight through it. I was glad to be on my own. A family of roos watched us coming on and kept their eyes on us till we was gone by. I turned around and looked back at them and they was still watching us, the big old father and the three mothers and two youngsters. They would not have seen too many horsemen passing that way and I dare say me and Mother was as good as a circus for them. I was taking a shortcut I knew but I was in no hurry to get back to the police house. I was having some time on my own. Which is the best company I know and you are most likely to win all the arguments. I thought about Ben and Deeds and their child and their happiness and I knew it was something good and important to our lives, the three of us, and that it was an advance on what we'd had before. There are times when it is right for things to change. I would be a proud uncle to their child and would do honour to them all in the best ways I could. It stood as a good thing in my future and made me think. I knew already I loved them three and I wondered at how it come about that suddenly Ben, my friend, was three people and my love for all of them three.

An hour's riding and me and Mother come on to the open ground where the Old People had their stone arrangements in the days before us whitefellers was around. The scrub come to a sudden end and that wide open space was shining white in the light of the stars in front of us. The starlight was always brighter over that playground. I do not know why that was. But it was something that always impressed me whenever I seen it. It made you stand and puzzle at it, and it made you know there was a lot of things in the life of the scrub you did not understand or have no knowledge of, even though you and your dad before you had spent your entire lives in it. Or almost entire.

Mother pulled up, her legs planted and her ears pointed at the shining space in front of us, her head up and a small trembling going through her. A horse has better eyes than a man and will see things a long way before a rider sees them. They speak to their rider with their ears. If Mother come to a stop it was always because she seen a reason for coming to a stop. She pulled up smartly one day when we was riding down a cattle pad to the water over by Coolan Creek when the hole was full and there was a mob gathered there. I waited with her till I saw what she was stopped for. A half minute later the biggest old-man king brown snake I ever seen crossed the track right there in front of us, his skin glistening in the sun with them rainbow colours they gets when they are in their breeding prime. I said in a quiet voice as that snake went past in front of us, It is as well to give those fellers room. There is not a horse nor any man would survive long the bite of one of them king browns when they are in their season. Anyway, that snake went on his way peacefully. They are the most aggressive snakes I know and it is likely he would not have given way to us, for they do not slip aside for people nor horses like other snakes do. I have wondered since then if Mother had some kind of vision of the future for herself in that meeting. It was the bite of a king brown killed her eventually. But that day she seen that big snake long before I seen him and she give him the right of way. He might have said to her, I will see you another day, old horse. She was not so old, but nearly everyone always called things old in them days even when they was not old. It was a way of marking them as something worthwhile. Now old means nothing but old.

Scrubber cattle had kicked over a lot of them stone patterns on the playgrounds, being curious of everything as they are, and had put them stones off their lines. But you could still see the patterns and arrangements in a general way. A dingo was starting up howling way back in the scrub behind us. That bitch probably had cubs and must have watched us going by like the roos had done but kept herself hid, then slipped in on our tracks and followed us some way. I do not know how them Old People treated that ground so the scrub never grew back on it and it shone the way it did, but they must have done something to it because it always stayed cleared. The secret for that was lost like a lot of things was lost. Them people from the coast think they know everything there is to know but I think we know less now than we did when my dad was a boy. That open ground did not shine the same in the day when the sun was on it, but only in the starlight. I sat a while looking over that sacred ground and I was aware I could know nothing of it. After a time I skirted around the rim and went on a hundred yards into the brigalow on the far side. I did not like to ride a horse across that open space.

There was a small natural clearing beside what we used to call the red wall. I knew a good waterhole in behind the red wall and I filled my quart pot there and set it on a fire and I squatted beside the fire and fed sticks around the quart until my tea water boiled. I had set Mother loose but she was not interested in feeding. She stood close, her head in the smoke, which was something she liked to do. She always seemed to know when there was something in the air and she never strayed too far. After my drink of tea I lay down with my jacket under my head and smoked a cigarette and looked up at the stars through a gap in the brigalow sticks above me. The moon was travelled over towards Coal Creek by then and the sky was clear and black, the stars rotating around me. I lay looking up for a long time thinking of them stars and my troubles come into my thoughts and what was coming to us, and I cherished the peace of that place I was in. My mother laid her hand on me and give me that sad little smile of hers. She said even though I was not addressing her Saviour, she seen I was at my prayers for the people I cared for. You do not need to speak direct to the Lord, she said, He knows when you are praying to Him.

There was an animal rattling among the dry ground litter off behind me towards the red wall. Mother raised her head and looked over that way. I always felt calm on my own in the scrub and I was in no hurry to get back to the police house. I liked to hear the animals doing their night business and not taking no notice of me. There was a peace in being there I could not have when I was in my bunk at my quarters. Each place has its own kind of peace and its own kind of trouble. And before I was done I was to know a place where no peace could ever exist for no one, except in death. But I will not speak of that here but will speak of it when the time comes to do so. I was thinking that night of being Uncle Bobby to Deeds and Ben's kid and how I was to have a family again, and maybe me and Irie would be together in that family one day and it would be the five of us. And who knows, maybe me and Irie would make it six of us. I was not thinking on death.

Someone was pushing at my shoulder and I woke out of my dream believing a stranger's hand touched me. Mother was nudging me with her nose. I sat up and put my hand on her nose and she backed off. Okay, I told her, we're going home now. I don't need you to start pushing me around. I could not remember my dream, only that I was at the small end of a tunnel and could see no way of turning this way or that but just had to keep going, the tunnel getting tighter around me the further I went. I believe there was someone with me but I do not know who it was; they was to my left and little more than a shadow to me. If I said it was Irie was with me I would be making it up. But I would not be surprised if it was Irie all the same. That is who I wanted it to be. But I will not say so for sure as I do not wish to make things up but only to tell the truth of this as I know it. I do not like such dreams and I stood up and shook it off. The moon was gone well over now and glinted low down through the scrub. I must have slept an hour or more. The fire was out, one ember sending up a last curl of smoke in the stillness. I left it to smoulder to its end. I felt more tired than I had before I slept. It seemed like we was coming to the end of something and I could not know what the future of it was to be. I felt I was on my own now. Which did not add up, but it was how I felt all the same. That was the feeling in me and I could see no reason for it. I tightened the girth and got up on Mother and she followed the red wall on a loose rein and I dozed in the saddle. I forget what I was thinking. But it would not have been much.

My father told me that red wall was one of them highways of the Old People when they come down to the great gatherings at the playgrounds. The rusty rock come up out of the ground at a leaning angle, as if some force under the ground was pushing it through, which I suppose it was. Every time we come by that way when I was a boy I expected to see the wall grown. In some places, at its highest, it was maybe eight or nine feet and in others it petered out entirely and went underground. I used to jump off my horse and measure myself against it to see if I had grown or the wall had grown. I said to my dad, How can it be a wall when it is underground? He said, That is what it is, Bobby. It is a wall.

I did not ask again. From nothing the wall will suddenly come up again and appear and disappear along a line through the scrub for some miles, maybe ten, like it is looking to take a breath of fresh air or to see where it is going. Them islands of red stone crop up out of the ground in isolated places, but if you know the country you know they are part of the same wall of natural rock continuing along a line that you may follow if you wish to, or cut off to one side of. You can always take your bearings by them isolated outcrops of red stone. I do not know the name of the stone. It would be in one of Daniel's books but I never felt like asking him. She goes underground and over the ground, and that is what I know. Which is what my dad meant. And I learned it from being there and without asking him nothing more. So he was right on both those counts. My dad was seldom wrong about things. He did not speak of things that he did not know himself. I never heard him speak of the Saviour as my mother did. I never did ask him directly, but I believe he had some private religion of his own. He respected my mother's beliefs and never said nothing against them. If you asked him a question and he did not know the answer to it he would tell you to attend to your work and that is all the answer you would get from him. He bore a strong contempt for people who carried an opinion on every subject. Dad and Ben's old man used to take their rum on the verandah of Chiller's away from the chatter at the bar. Dad kept his greatest affection for my mother. A smile between them two would fill a book with meanings.

Mother propped suddenly under me and I opened my eyes and looked around me. I said, What do you see, old girl? She stood her ground, letting me know she had seen something worth stopping for. It took me a while to pick it but then I seen the horse tracks across a patch of starlit dirt just out in front of us. I got down and had a close look at them and I knew it was old Finisher must have come that way. It was me put them shoes on him myself only days ago and I would know my own work anywhere. I did not think it would have been Daniel finding his bearings through the brigalow by the red wall but Finisher deciding on getting home the best way he could. Daniel would have been bushed by now over this way, I was confident of that. I followed Finisher's tracks for some time until I seen where they struck off to the east, following a line that would cut the Mount Hay road after a mile or so. I did not go on there but angled off until I struck the wall again. I did not need the wall to know where I was but it was the way I chose to ride. I was sure Finisher would have got Daniel home to the police house. I would see in the morning if Daniel was going to admit he had been lost or would he keep quiet about it. I looked forward to testing him on it. Daniel always put himself up as a very upright man and made it clear he did not believe in lies.

I heard him tell Irie more than once, Lies will get you nowhere in this world, young lady. When Daniel spoke to her in that tone Irie's lovely face went ugly and closed up, her mouth set in a stiff line and her eyes kind of fixed with a look of disdain in them that would have made Daniel feel the chill if he had seen it, which he may have done. I could see Irie was going to be a strong woman to deal with when she was grown up. She was already strong but she kept her strength to herself. I had an idea she was a pretty good liar when she knew the truth was going to get her in trouble. Lies have their place in all our lives. Good lies and bad. We would see how Daniel was to go with this one, if he was to lie or maybe half lie by not telling us the whole story, which to me is worse than a full lie and speaks of a weakness in a man to know truth from lies. The man who deals in half-lies cannot be trusted when the pressure is on but will go the way that seems to him the easiest way to go. I seen it often. I enjoyed thinking about fronting Daniel on this. Irie would be watching her dad as closely as I would be and she and I would share our understanding of how things was going with one of them private looks we give each other. I did enjoy them private looks between me and Irie more than I can tell you. Words is not much use for the real things of our lives. We know inside us what we know.

. . .

Tip did not bark when I rode out from the timber but come across from under the tank stand and greeted me and Mother down at the yards. I took the gear off Mother and give her a rub down with the saddle cloth and I took her out a scoop of oats and turned her off into the horse paddock. The other horses come up to see if they might get something of what she was getting and Mother laid back her ears and sooled them off.

I went over to my quarters and took off my clothes and got myself under my blanket. I could not sleep but lay there feeling like the blood was draining out of my body. My strength and my hopes for things running out of me. A kind of exhaustion took me over and I felt like I weighed half a ton, the springs of that cot sagging under the pressure of my body. I never felt like that before. I could not sleep with the thoughts that was going around in my head like lightning flickering in the ranges, and I cannot tell you now what them thoughts was. They was not my thoughts but was the thoughts of something I did not understand. Lying there it was like I was spinning inside and had no strength left to stop the spinning. I knew it was a loneliness that was come on me. I never felt that out in the scrubs. Tip come tap-tapping her claws onto my narrow verandah and she laid her head on her paws and looked in at me, them beautiful eyes of hers glinting in the darkness with the kindness in her. I told her, I do not feel too good. But I cannot tell you why, old girl, I said. She listened to me the way a dog will listen to you, her eyebrows and ears twitching, signalling her feelings. It may be true that dogs have no thoughts. But there is no arguing against a dog having feelings. Which is another matter. My dad would not have had an opinion on it.

When the rooster woke me from my sleep with his flapping and crowing it was already full daylight, the heat coming through them thin fibro walls of my quarters. I sat up, my dreams slipping out of my mind and going to wherever they go to when we have done with them. Tip was gone off the verandah and I knew Irie would have already been out to feed the chooks, which was her first chore of the day before she got ready for school. Irie did not usually look in at me, because I was always up and about the place before she was, but I wondered if she might have just peeked around my door this morning. I had an uneasy feeling in me and I could not shake it. I got up and put on my moleskins and shirt and I pulled on my boots and pushed my hat on and I went out off the verandah and walked over to the police house.

Esme was at the stove frying eggs, and Irie and Miriam was sitting at the table eating their cereal. The three of them looked at me as I come through the flywire door. Miriam give Irie a squinty look, pouting and being her usual discontented self. It was always surprising to me that Irie was never cross with that sister of hers but always looked after her and was careful with her feelings. I would not have had Irie's patience for it. I seen Miriam give Irie a hit with her hand once, real hard and mean, and a look of pain went across Irie's face but she did nothing in return. I heard kids say Irie seen herself as her sister's champion down at the school too. That is the way it was between them two, the older child looking after the younger child. It is not always so and was not so with me and Charley. Esme smiled at me and said, Good morning, sleepy head, and she dished up my breakfast and told me to sit down and eat my corned beef and eggs while the eggs was still hot. Cold eggs are not good for your digestion, she said.

I seen Esme was not going to say nothing to me about how she had been wrong to carry on about Rosie's accusations the way she did, but was going to act to me as if all that never happened. The truth is the truth. If we say it or not we all know it. I was disappointed in her with this and I wondered if she still believed we was friends. She had not asked me to read to her for a while and I had noticed that. I thanked her for the breakfast and I said, Who is painting the cupboards? Esme said, Do you like the colour? The kitchen cupboard doors was all open and there was a smell of paint. The cans and china plates and other stuff that had been in the cupboards was laid out on the bench tops. The cupboards was half painted a hard blue. It was bluer than any sky I ever seen. They had been a dull old scratched-up green before. I said I liked the colour well enough. Irie laughed at me saying this. Bobby means he hates it, Mum, she said and she looked across at me and we both looked at each other with one of them looks that says to each other what we are not saying to no one else. A rush of feeling went through me when I seen that look in her eyes and my stomach turned over. I had to take a drink of tea to get my breakfast out of the way. There was no one else could ever do that to me the way Irie could do it. I felt my face colouring up and hoped Esme would not notice. Irie was laughing, seeing the effect she was having on me, and Miriam was looking pure hatred at me. I did not care about Miriam. Mum's going to paint the walls bright green when she's finished with the cupboards, Irie said. I seen she was in a mood to have some fun.

Esme come over and sat down with her own breakfast. She took a drink of tea and looked around the kitchen as if everything was calm in her world and just the way she liked it to be. Esme was happy being the boss of her world. Well, she said, things needed freshening up in here and I could see your father was never going to get around to doing it. It sounded to me like she had decided they was going to stay here and make their life in Mount Hay after all, now she had no fear of a brutal killer of young women and girls on the loose out in the scrub. I said nothing. I liked Esme Collins in a number of ways and she was a strong woman herself, and that was something you had to admire. But I suppose it was more or less at that moment that I decided she did not know how to understand people who was not like her. I never had no cause later on to change my judgment on that. It come to me and I knew it. And it surprised me. She was not unkind but was generous and helpful. At the back of her mind I knew she did not see me as an equal to her and her family. And I guess I resented that. It is an easy thing to resent. I wished my own mother had been around to correct her. But that could not be. My dad would have had no time for Esme Collins but would have left her to herself. I knew that, but I was not as clear on these things as Dad was and I always looked for the best in people, and wanted to believe that deep down they was good. My dad would have been scornful of that idea.

I was eating my breakfast and thinking these thoughts when I felt the touch of Irie's school shoe pressing against the side of my boot. She pushed until I looked at her. Her lips was twisted into a shape that was half smile and half something else that I cannot put a name to. Her eyes was hard and glittery, as if she expected me to say something to her out in the open in front of her mother and sister. She was scaring me. I never seen her look that way before.

She pressed hard on my boot until she forced me to move my foot away. My heart was whipping around in my chest and my cheeks was hot, half with fear and half with the excitement of it. Esme seen there was something going on with me and she looked hard at me. Oh! she said. Now I am so sorry, Bobby! I forgot again to leave the fat on your corned beef. I'm afraid I gave it to Tip. I could see she was laughing and was not too upset with herself for cutting the fat off my corned beef. She would not have been laughing if she could have seen what was going on under her kitchen table just then with her husband's offsider and her daughter.

Irie had never been so direct before. It was a new turn in our friendship. I was not sure if we could ever get ourselves back to where we had stood before, without being called on to do something about this new turn. Which I had no intention of doing. I feared Irie might not be going to let me go on treating her like a child but was going to insist on something else between us. Whatever that something else was she had in mind. If she had anything in mind. Which I do not suppose she did have with any clearness, but only the feelings of it, which was strong in her just then. The way I seen it Irie Collins was still a child at that time and that is how I wished things to go on between us. I give Irie a hard look, like I was her teacher, and I cleared my throat and said, That is okay, Mrs Collins. She put her hand on mine and said to Irie and Miriam, Oh dear, I've upset our Bobby now, I can see that. I wanted to tell her, I am not your Bobby, Mrs Collins. I am my own Bobby and no one else's. But I let it go.

Daniel come through from the police office. Like always he was wearing a fresh ironed shirt and had had a shave, his hair slicked down, his belt leather shining and the police buckle so polished it looked like it had just been issued to him. He seen me sitting there and he said good morning and went over to the sink and washed his hands. He did not say nothing of Ben and Deeds or about him calling the Dawsons on the telephone. I was expecting him to ask me how I had gone out there with Ben and Deeds. But it all just clung there between us in his silence, like old mud hard and cracked and needing to be picked off as soon as ever we could get to it. Irie said, Dad got lost coming home through the scrub from Coal Creek. I looked at Daniel. He shook the water off his hands and wiped them on a tea towel and he turned around and smiled at her. It's nice you're sticking up for your old dad, darling, he said. Miriam did not look at me but I knew it was me she was talking to when she said, My dad did not get lost. That stupid old horse of his got lost and Dad found his way home. Irie give a bit of a snort at this and wiped the yellow streaks of yolk off her plate with a piece of toast and ate it. There was a kind of impatience in her way of doing this that I did not think rightly belonged to the manners of a child. Daniel stood behind Esme's chair and he said, As usual the truth is somewhere between the two of you. He leaned down and kissed Esme on her cheek and she went to get up and he put his hand to her shoulder and said it was okay, he would get his own breakfast. But Esme made him sit down and she left her breakfast to get cold and got up and put his eggs on to fry. Cooking was her territory and she was not giving it up that easily. He come over and sat on my right-hand side and started telling the girls to get a hurry on or they would be late for school, just as if there was nothing between him and me that needed talking about.

. . .

I went down to the yards and give my gear a going-over with the mixture I had made up for the harness. Daniel come down later and he told me to take the jeep and go and tell Rosie Gnapun we had located Deirdre and she was okay. I said, Deeds is more than okay. Her and Ben is having a baby. Daniel said, Well, I am pleased to hear it. But he did not sound too pleased.

I took the jeep and headed out for Rosie's place. As I was driving down to find Rosie the thought come to me that Irie had showed something of that same old feeling as Ben's in her mood at breakfast, going with her feelings and not knowing how far she was going with them. And maybe frightening herself with how the feelings was getting hold of her, like a horse that is too strong and too wild for its rider and is stirred up by the touch on the bit. That look in her eyes frightened me, that I do know. I had always been the boss of my own feelings until I met Irie. Before that I truly believed we was born one way or the other. I do take after my mother in this more than my father and I am not like Ben. I seen my father lose his temper with people, but never with animals, and I never seen my mother get too carried away at all, and there were times she had plenty of cause to. Usually my dad was quiet, but it was a quiet you was careful around. I had seen Ben softened with Deeds and the thought of their child, and I did not know whether to think that people never do change all the way through or that they do change. How was I to know either way? My head was just full of questions and I had no answers for them. I was thinking so hard on these things I drove clean past the turn-off to the town camp and had to spin around and come on back along the road in my own dust.

. . .

When the girls come home from school later in the day I went over to the house for my reading and writing lesson with Irie. I did not know how it would be with her. But she was quiet and thoughtful

and did not play up like she had in the morning. I had the feeling
things was not the same as they had been with us, but saw she
was holding it in now and considering it. That girl was neither
a child nor a woman at that time of her life but was on the edge
of strong things in herself that was new to her and she did not
have the way of them yet. I seen it was that time when we make
some stupid mistakes that we live to regret. Sitting beside her at
the kitchen table doing the reading lesson I got the feeling from
her she was alone with herself and with the puzzle of her strong
feelings of that morning. She was not sharing herself with Miriam
the way she usually did. Which was another cause for Miriam to
hate me all the harder. I was wishing things could go on being
just the same as before. But that was not going to happen. I was
either going to have to ride it to its end or get off right that minute
and clear out. I could not bring myself to do that. I valued it too
much. Maybe it would have been better if I had cut the tie right
then. I have come to know since that day that we can recover from
just about any loss in this life but the loss of life itself.

Esme was up on a chair painting the cupboards and singing to
herself and Miriam was doing her homework at the other end of
the table. Miriam kept looking up from her work to ask questions
of Irie. Irie had patience with her sister and she interrupted our
reading lesson and come back to Miriam with an answer every

time. I caught Miriam's look and seen how she was smirking at interrupting the lesson for me. Irie and me was reading from her school book. It was a story about a man in the old days. His ship sank in the sea and his mates was all lost and drowned. He was the only one to make it to an island. I forget the name of that book. I did not believe the truth of it and did not think much of it. We had the book open between us on the table and Irie read a piece first, following her reading with her finger so I could follow it too. Then I read the piece over after her and she asked me if I knew what this or that word meant. I copied down with a pencil on a piece of paper the words I did not know. I had to take this list of words to my quarters and learn them off by heart later. Which I mostly did as I wished to be a good reader, and for Irie to admire me for it, which was more than half my reason for doing it. And I liked her to feel she was a good teacher too. If I come on a word I could not read out, Irie leaned close and whispered to me how to say it, as if she was whispering a secret between us. And I knew this is just what she was doing. And she knew it too. I asked her to repeat a word and we both smiled at this, knowing what I was up to. Miriam was on the lookout and yelled, Mum! Irie and Bobby are whispering again. Esme stopped her painting and turned around and said, That is not nice, Miriam. Irie is whispering a word to Bobby so she will not disturb your work by speaking it aloud. Please be nice to Bobby. Miriam made a face at me. I did not mind her. I winked back at her so she would hate me all the harder. It was easy to make her cry and I knew I could do that if I wished to and she knew it too. I kept it so she was just a little bit afraid of what I might do if she stirred me up too much. This way I kept her on the chain. I knew I could not keep Irie on no chain. If anyone was on Irie's chain it was me. Them things are the way they are and it is no good us fighting them.

Irie was reading to me how the man on the island picks up the tracks of another man and sees he is not alone. Her voice was soft and serious, her head close to mine. It made me very happy to be so close to her and her not doing nothing wild. I listened to her reading and I thought of my mother reading her Bible out loud in the evening to me and Dad when we was home from the camps, which she did almost every evening. My dad could not read neither. He never tried to learn. While Mum read her Bible my dad used to go to sleep by the fire after a time. But I never did. I watched my mother's face and saw in her eyes the great meaning them words in the Bible had for her. My dad had no shame of not being able to read. If something needed reading when we come into Mount Hay he asked someone to read it for him. But that did not happen very often. Mostly he got by okay without needing to read. There was nothing ever needed reading in the scrubs. And he could read the scrubs without trying. My mother had a good education off the nuns in reading and writing and in singing. I still had her old Bible. I kept it beside my bunk in the drawer of the cupboard that was there. It was wrapped in an old red silk scarf of hers. When I balled the scarf in my hand and held it to my nose and closed my eyes I could smell her hair. Her smell lingered in that scarf for years after she passed away. I sat on the side of my bed some nights and got out her Bible and opened it on my knees and turned the pages. It was a very small Bible, not much bigger than the palm of my hand, and the pages was so thin you could have rolled cigarettes with them. I could not read it yet, the writing was so small and so many of the words were not known to me, but I hoped to be able to read it one day with Irie's help. I had whole sections of it by heart from hearing my mother read them to me many times. Her favourite parts was in the Book of Revelation.

I was listening to Irie reading the story of the man on the island and I was thinking these thoughts about my mother and her Bible when Irie leaned in close to me so her forehead touched my cheek just for a moment before she pulled back. She whispered, I do not get lost in the scrubs, Bobby. I was surprised and I looked at her. I seen how serious she was in making this claim and I did not laugh at her. She was shining with it. I whispered back to her, Everyone gets lost once, Irie. Like I heard you only get homesick once. She did not say nothing to this for a minute but thought about it. Then she said in a whisper, Did you ever get lost in the scrubs? I said I did, but only once. And did you ever get homesick? she wanted to know. I said I had never been away from the ranges but I would be sure to get sick pining for them if I ever did leave.

PART TWO

EIGHT

I was deep asleep that night and content in my dreams, the moon shining through my door as it always did, when I was woken up by a tapping on my fingers where my hand was hanging out over the side of the bunk. It was a strange soft kind of tap-tap-tap, like a child might tap at a sleeping dog to test if it is still alive, half scared to wake the dog but curious to see. I woke up and pulled my hand away. Irie was crouching beside my bunk in her pyjama shorts and top. She was barefoot and her hair was all tossed around and sticking out from her head. In the day Irie always kept her hair well brushed and I had often admired its shine. I was very startled to see her there and I sat up and said, Jesus, Irie! You had better get back to your bed before your mother comes looking for you.

I will be sacked and thrown off the place if they catch you out here with me. She had never done nothing like this before. She stood up and stepped away from my bunk, like she was afraid I was going to make a grab at her. I said, Whoa! I am not going to grab you.

She said, I did not think you were going to grab me, and I don't know why you say that. Her voice was kind of breathless, and I suppose it was with the fear and the excitement of what she was daring herself to. She said, We can never talk about interesting things over at the house with Miriam spying on us all the time, only whisper them. I want you to know how good I am in the bush, Bobby, but I never get the chance to show you. I may not yet be as good as you are, but I will be just as good as you one day. I never get lost like Dad. I always find my way. As she talked she was settling down to it and the boldness come back into her voice. You don't think too much of me as a bushman, she said, I know that. You never say anything to me about it. But I want you to know I am just as good a bushman as you are a reader. I tell you all the time what a good reader you are and I know you like to hear me say that.

I had never thought of looking at things this way between us and I laughed at the idea of her admiring me for being a bushman. Being at home in the bush was just the way I was from when I was a kid. What else was I? The scrubs was my home like they had been home for my dad and Ben and for everyone who worked them. I did not think of myself as a bushman but just as me. And I did not consider being as I was to be anything special for anyone but myself. She said with a sharpness in her voice, Don't you laugh at me, Bobby Blue! I never laughed at you when you were first trying to read. I always helped you. I will prove to you how good I am if you will come with me and let me show you something in the scrub. She looked at me a minute, considering something. Then she said, That is if you are not too scared of my mother. She stood waiting to see what I was going to say to this, ready to despise me if I showed my fear of her mother, who she did not fear. I could not see her expression with the moonlight behind her through the open door, but I heard in her voice she was determined and I knew she was not about to have her mind changed with no arguments from me. I said, Well, Irie Collins, I guess I am as game for anything as you are. But you will have to go out on the verandah there and wait for me while I get my pants and shirt on.

It was the most foolish thing I was ever likely to do in my entire life, but I went on with it anyway. I never once felt scared climbing onto one of them black bulls in the chute at the Mount Hay rodeo when they used to have it out there, but I was trembly in my legs now and had to sit on the side of the bed to get my feet through the legs of my pants. There was two people in me: the steady one who was always the boss of his own feelings and the other one who did not care what was going to happen but was going to ride this thing whichever way it was to turn out. I could not put down the excitement in me. It was too strong for putting down. We are different in the night to how we are in the day. The night makes us someone else and we believe our daylight self will not see us and we can keep our night self secret from our day self. That is why the night is when evil is done, and the morning is for repentance and remorse. What I was doing following Irie scared me, but I still climbed out of my bunk and pulled on my pants and shirt and pulled on my boots. I could see her sitting on the verandah, swinging her legs over the side and talking to Tip, who had come out to see what was going on. Sitting there swinging her legs Irie was only just coming up to thirteen in a month or two and I was already past my twentieth birthday and a full-grown working man at that time. I should have told her to go on back to bed and to find a way of showing me the secret she wanted to show me in the morning. Which is what my mother would have approved in me and I knew it. I did not think it would have been too hard for Irie and me to find ways of meeting and talking in the day if we had looked to do it. I knew what I was doing was wrong and would not be approved of by any grown-ups except maybe Ben, who would have laughed at the idea of it if he had known of it.

There was something I did not think much of at the time, and it is only looking back now that I see how close this whole thing was for me and Irie that night, and how it all hung on that one small detail. I see it now, but at the time I brushed it aside and thought nothing of it. It was this. Daniel never put Tip on the chain at night like anyone from Mount Hay, who would always chain their dogs, because Esme would not allow it. And if Tip had been on the chain she would have barked and rattled her chain when she seen Irie sneaking out to my quarters in her pyjamas in the dead of night. Then Daniel would have come out to see what was upsetting his dog and the whole thing that come out of this night would not have gone on to happen and all our lives would have been different. That is why a dog is on a chain in Mount Hay, so it will do its job and warn you when there is something unusual going on. Being off the chain, Tip thought she would join the party. I looked at that dog and I said to myself, None of this would be happening if Daniel was from the ranges and was not a coastal man. That was my thought. And I was amused by it, and it did not put me on my guard as it should have done, like it was the warning that come to me instead of the barking of the dog coming to Irie's dad. I ignored the warning and just laughed at it. Tip looking up at Irie with that eagerness for adventure, her tail slapping from side to side like she was signalling me, only I was refusing to see the meaning of her signal. Refusing to see it because I did not want to see it. So does that make me responsible for the tragedy that come to us from these small beginnings? That is a question I have asked myself many times since. It is a question everyone else asked themselves too, except Esme, who did not ask anything of herself but only of other people. For Esme I was always to be the villain who had betrayed her and her family. She never shifted on that once it was fixed in her mind.

I went out onto the verandah and Irie got up and stood to face me, the moonlight white and clear, the clean pale light of it shining on her, the pinpoints of the moon in her eyes. And I seen she was just as eager as Tip for this night adventure. I said, I will come with you if you will go and get your jeans and a shirt on. I am not going into the scrub with you wearing them shortie pyjamas. She looked down at herself. I am warm enough, she said. I said, I do not care if you are warm or cold. That is not my point. She looked up at me and said, If I go back I might wake up Miriam. I said, That is a risk you will have to take. You already took a risk coming out here, so I believe you can take that risk as well. I am not coming with you if you do not do as I am asking you to do. She stood a while looking back at me and I thought she was going to stay stubborn on her decision. In my fear I was seeing Miriam waking up and finding her sister gone and going into her mother and father's bedroom and telling them, and Esme and Daniel coming out to look for Irie, calling her name and flashing torches around the way they did even when there was a moon to see by. I did not wish to be found hanging about in the scrub at night with their daughter wearing only them cotton shorts and that top with one button holding it together. If we was to be found I wanted Irie to be properly dressed in her clothes. That would be bad enough, but not as bad as the other. I said, You had better decide right now. I am not budging on this one.

She said nothing but jumped off the verandah and ran back along the path past the hen run, Tip flying along behind her. And that is when Tip let out a bark of excitement. I thought, Well that is it then, that yelping will have woken them up. I felt a mix of regret and relief that I would not be having this night adventure with Irie after all. I stood on my verandah looking over towards the back steps to the police house, and I waited. I was half hoping to see Irie running back along the path to me and half hoping not to see her. But I was not strong enough in my mind to know for sure where I wanted to be with it. I knew where I should be with it, but that was different to deciding to be there. Knowing is not wanting or deciding. I was all off-balance, like a man with one foot in the stirrup and one foot free when his horse gets a scare and takes off with him. I knew it could go either way for me just then. I went back inside and I put my hat on and got my tobacco and I come out onto the verandah again and rolled a cigarette and lit it. The smoke did not settle my nerves.

I seen her coming back then, Tip at her heels. She had on her jeans and boots and a check shirt she wore. I watched her walking towards me through the moonlight and I said aloud to myself, My God, Irie Collins. Just look at you. And I knew just what I meant saying her name aloud in this admiring way, but I cannot put the words to that meaning here. There was something in it of my amazement at her trusting me. I had never met no one like her. I stepped off the verandah and said to her, You did not wake Miriam then? She said, Mirri was snoring. She snores like an old man. We walked down to the horse paddock and I held the barb back for her to climb through the wire and when she was through she turned around and held it for me and I ducked and went through it. I straightened up and said, I seen you and Miriam slipping off into the scrub down here one night. She said, very grown up, I know you did.

We went on without saying more. She was not a chatterbox. We climbed through the wire at the far end of the paddock, the horses watching us, and went on into the scrub. I wondered if Irie was as nervous as I was. She did not show no nerves if she had them. She was an unusual young woman. I believe she always was. I could not see that she belonged to this family, but just belonged to herself. Miriam must have been ten going on for eleven around then but she always seemed to me like a much younger kid than her age. Miriam did not know herself as Irie knew herself and needed to look to her mother to be told how she was going. Irie looked to herself. She knew how she was going. It was not something you could teach but was bred in them two girls, one way or the other. It was what made them different, even though they was close sisters. Irie was not the leader between them because she was older than Miriam. She was the leader because that is what she was. A leader. I have seen people in life who wish to be the leader and others who are the leader without caring one way or another about being it. That was Irie Collins. She was a natural born leader. You either followed her or you stayed behind.

She took the lead with me that night and I was content to follow along, watching her going through the scrub a couple of steps ahead of me, taking me to her secret place. Light and quick she was, like a moon shadow herself, flickering through the bendee. I believe she was afraid of nothing. She was not following a cattle pad but ducked and weaved her way with a clear notion of where she was heading. We had gone on somewhat over a mile when we come to a clearing. There was some kind of stick shelter. She stopped and turned to me and said, See? Here it is. I can find my way in the dark. She looked at me, expecting praise from me, I dare say, for finding her way without ever stopping to check. We stood side by side looking at the shelter. I said, You did that very well. She said, Thank you. That is the first time you ever said anything nice to me about my ability in the scrub. I said, Well, you do have it and I have always seen you had it, but I never thought to say nothing to you about it. But it is because I trust you in such things that I give you Mother to ride instead of that old plug of your dad's. She said, You are not the only one in the world who likes to hear a word of praise, Bobby Blue. I have heard you compliment your horse at the end of a long day. I said, I am sorry. I was not thinking. I will tell you in the future if there are things about you I admire. She said, I would like that. We looked at each other and we was both laughing and it seemed suddenly to be kind of strange that I was saying this to her standing out there in the scrub in the middle of the night. She said, I would like you to tell me those things that you admire about me when you think of them. Please don't keep them to yourself. I'm glad you think I am capable in the bush. I would not like you to believe me to be a fool.

I knew what she was aiming at and I said, Your dad is a good man in his heart and he is honest. I have met a lot worse than him. You are lucky to have a good father. She come back at me, I know that. Dad understands me in ways Mum never will and I love him. But he lets himself be told by Mum and I would like to see him stand up to her. Dad is never going to be a real bushman and you know that as well as I do. He is a fool in the bush. That is all I meant. I am being honest, that is all, I am not being mean.

I was glad to let it go at that as I did not want to be wasting our good feelings talking about Daniel with her at that moment. The shelter was made of dry brigalow sticks closely put together, with leaves and pieces of rusted tin. It was built up against an isolated island of the red wall, where the wall comes out of the ground. I knew the place well but had not been by that way for some time. The cattle dung I had seen was all old and grey and broken about. I seen no tracks of cattle all the way out and the pad we crossed had only dog and roo tracks on it. Tip was at the entrance to the shelter, nose to the ground, snuffling. Irie invited me to step inside with her and she went down on her knees and disappeared into the dark of the shelter. I got down on my knees and crawled in after her. There was not a lot of room and we was bumping around on each other getting settled. Tip stayed at the door. Irie struck a match and put it to the wick of a candle she had stuck to the bottom of an empty tuna in brine can. She set the candle between us on the ground and we sat cross-legged like Red Indians in their teepee, the small yellow flame between us reaching and flickering and lighting her face. She had her back leaning against the red stone of the wall island. I said, You are not afraid of being out here on your own in the night, then? She said, Miriam is scared of being here. I'm not. Miriam is even scared of being alone in our room at night. I said, That may be, but them bull ants out here can give you a lift. She said, There are no bull ants just here where I am sitting. I said, They will find you. I seen she was getting just a bit cocky with it and it made me smile. I said, One of these days you are going to come face to face with some old scrubber bull and that will stop you in your tracks.

She was fussing around with getting the lid off a tin and I sat admiring her. Your mother did not notice you stole a candle from her? I said. I stole it from school, she said. They don't notice anything at school. I have lots of them here. She got the lid off the tin and held it out to me. I looked in it. There was some dates and pieces of broken biscuit. She smiled when I looked at her. It is more fun being here with you than with Miriam. You don't complain all the time. I took a piece of broken biscuit and a date and thanked her. I said, If Miriam is scared in her own room while you are there with her, if she wakes up and finds you gone, what about that? Irie shrugged her narrow shoulders and offered me another go at the biscuit tin. She did not wish to think of the worst any

more than I did. We sat eating our biscuits and the dried dates.
I said, That lid must be tight. Them little black ants would like
these dates if they could get into them. She considered the lid but
said nothing. The night was deep and quiet.

Tip whimpered and pushed her backside in the entrance. Irie
said, Tip is afraid. I said, Tip hears a dingo howling up in them
stone escarpments. Irie said, Can you hear it? No, I said, I cannot.
The dog can hear more than we can. We sat a while in silence
eating our dates and biscuits. Now we was free and alone together
it seemed like we could not think of nothing to say to each other.
But I did not mind if we said nothing at all. It was just good being
there with her. I looked at her sitting in the light of that school
candle, cross-legged and eating them dates and broken biscuits, and
I wondered what I thought I was doing out there in the middle of
the night with this girl. I could make no sense of what I expected
to come of it. But there was something firm in me that was going
on with it to wherever it was going to take us. It was more precious
to me than anything else I had. I knew that. I felt blessed by her
trust in me. And it was like her mother and father and the police
house and the rest of Mount Hay did not exist, and it was just
Irie and me out there on our own in the night and was no one's
business but ours that we was there together. I would keep her

safe no matter what, like in my daze of the fire. I would fly with her if I had to.

She said, You promised to tell me about the time you got bushed. I said, I will tell you something right now about your shelter here that is more interesting than me getting lost in the scrub when I was a boy. You see that red stone you are leaning against? She squirmed around and looked at the stone face and placed the flat of her hand on it. Me and Miriam decided this is a magic stone, she said. I said, And you are right. There is the spirits of the Old Murri people all around here. I told her about the line of isolated outcrops of the red wall leading from here to the playgrounds of the Old Murri people. I said, Them Murris called the red wall their highway and when the strangers gathered there for meetings they knew the wall from hearing of it even though they had never seen it before and they followed it where it led them. It was always a feature of their knowledge maps. And it was like a welcome when they seen this first little outcrop sticking up. And this is it, I said. This first outcrop of the wall is where you made your shelter. You are right to say there is a magic in it. Right here where you set your camp and are resting your back. There is no better place than this to camp out here.

She reached around and touched the stone of the wall again and said nothing. I was proud of her for her silence, for I could see she had a strong feeling for the story of the red wall I had given her. Learning that she had set her camp in a place like that was something I understood would mean a great deal to her. And I believed she would not talk about it as if it was nothing to her. It was a story first given me by my father. Dad knew some of them Old Murris of this part of the ranges when he was a boy, and they trusted him with some of their knowledge. I told her how the playgrounds shone like a white silk dress in the starlight but was dull under a full moon and that it was a mystery to know why this was. The means of making ground shine like that has been lost, I said. When I was finished telling her she said, Will you take me there tonight? I said, Well, it is too far. We would not be home before light. I should like to go there, she said.

She sat considering me for some time, chewing on a date. She took the date stone out of her mouth and looked at it. It glistened in the candlelight with her spit. She set the stone down and looked at me and did not look away. She said, You always have a reason for not doing things. I said, Like what else haven't I done? You promised to take me to the spring of the fig tree one day. I said, And I will do that when we have the chance for it. That old tree is not going nowhere and it will still be there when we get to it. It is best to wait till the signs are right before you try to do something like that. Or you are just pushing against things and they do not work out as you hope they will. If you and me was to go to the spring of the fig tree now your father would wish to come with us. She said, That is true. She stared at me a long while until I got uncomfortable with it. I said, What is it? She said, I am wondering if you are one of those people who keep their promises. Or if you are one of those people who find reasons for breaking their promises. I did not like to hear this. I said, Well, you will find that out one way or another in time, and then you will have the answer to your question. She asked me then, Do you think the signs are right for us? I did not know what to say to this. I believed in my heart all the real signs was right between us, but I did not trust our situation to work out in our favour. So I said nothing and her question hung there and she was not upset I did not answer her. She knew our situation just as well as I did.

We was silent a while after this. I rolled a smoke and lit it and I blew the smoke out the entrance. She said in a quiet voice, I like the smell of your cigarette, Bobby. You don't have to blow the smoke out the door. I looked at her and she smiled and said, I did not mean to say I do not trust you. I believe we are friends and can say anything that is in our minds to each other. And that is what being friends is. I said, I believe that too. You know how to speak your mind straight out better than I do. I will learn that from you. We both laughed and she said she was glad she had not upset me. I told her it would be hard for her to do that. I thought about it and said, We cannot know everything there is to know about each other yet. She said, Do you think we ever will? I said, Know everything about each other? Yes, she said. I knew that my dad would not have answered a question like that. I said, I do not think we can ever know that, but I do think we can trust each other. I was thinking how much I knew of Ben and yet I knew nothing of him really when it come to being sure of what was in his mind. After this Irie and me began to talk more openly about ourselves and our lives and the things we was hoping for. I cannot remember now what them things was that we talked about but I know they seemed important and true to us at the time. The pleasure was not in the things but was in sharing with each other. And that I do remember. The candle burned down and we forgot the time that was going by.

. . .

Irie Collins was the first friend I ever had outside Ben Tobin. And the first woman friend I ever had. If I can call her that. She would have liked me calling her a woman, I know that, even though she was not really at that stage of her life just yet. As well as teaching me how to read and write she taught me a lot about friendship and how we can talk to each other in ways I never thought of before, and how we can ask each other questions and disagree without getting angry or impatient. I knew it was dangerous, me and her being friends and being out there together. But I did not wish to put a name to how I felt about her, or to speak with her of the danger to myself. I did not see there was also a danger in it to her. I only come to that understanding later on. We do not see everything at once.

Tip was settled in the doorway of the shelter, her snout resting on her paws, which was crossed under her chin. She give a woof and sat up. Me and Irie both looked out at the night. I seen the sky was getting light over to the east and I said, We had better be getting back. Irie said, Is someone coming? I said, Tip was just letting us know it is time to be getting back. If Miriam wakes up she will see you are gone and will tell your parents. Irie said, If Miriam wakes up and I am not there with her she will be too scared to get out of her bed in case the monster that hides under her bed grabs her by the ankle. I said, Well we had better be getting back all the same, or they will be up and about before we are there. Irie said, I would not care too much if they did find out about us. Would you? I said, Then I would be out of a job and you and me would not be able to see each other. She said, I would run away if they tried to stop me seeing you. She looked at me very serious then and she said, I want to be a woman of the ranges, just as you are a man of the ranges. This is more my country than the coast ever was. I don't want to go back there. I feel as if I have known this place all my life. That is how I have felt since the day we got here. That first day, before we unpacked anything and I was standing at the back door for the first time looking out at the scrub and the distant escarpments, I said to Mum, There is a funny feeling about this place. She thought I was going to tell her I didn't like it. But I said, It feels as if this place is already our home. She said to me, Well that's lovely, darling. Mount Hay is going to be our home for a while, so I'm very glad you feel like that. But that was not what I meant. I meant I knew it here. When I first looked out on it from the back door of the police house I felt as if I already knew this country and it was my home country. Mum didn't understand. She never does. She thinks I'm still a child. I said to her, I meant, it feels as if we have come home. She didn't take any notice of this but asked me to give her a hand unpacking the kitchen things so we could get a meal underway. The kids at the school are the same. They only talk about getting away to the coast. They hate Mount Hay and the scrub. Most of them have never been into the scrub. They don't want to go into it. All they ever talk about is getting down to the coast and into the city when they finish school and buying a car. But this is where I want to be. She was frowning with the heaviness of her thoughts. You are the only one who understands what I feel about the ranges. She looked at me in a way that made me feel I had better not betray her trust in me, not ever. I did not say nothing for some time, but I had liked to hear her say I was the only one who understood her. I was thinking of myself at her age of thirteen and how I believed myself to be a man and had been working in the team with my dad and Ben and his dad for three years by that age. When I did not say nothing she said, And I do not want to get you sacked. She wet two fingers with her tongue and snuffed out the candle.

We crawled out of the shelter and I let her take the lead through the scrub, as I seen she was keen to do that. The moon had gone down behind Mount Dennison and the air was cold, the bendee whispering with the coming dawn, the birds chattering nervously waiting for the light to break free of the night before getting their courage up. Walking behind Irie there was a sadness in me that one day me and that girl would most likely have to go our own separate ways.

NINE

Some days went by, it might have been a week or longer, I do not remember the exact amount of time. Me and Daniel was busy with a bunch of fresh-branded cows that turned up in the Mount Hay yards. Someone told Frank Dawson about the cows and he come into town and stopped the sale going ahead. He claimed they was cleanskins robbed off his country a while back and fresh branded with some Territorian's new brand, which was not familiar to none of us in Mount Hay. There was only thirty of them cows and they was so poor-looking I did not think they was worth troubling about, but Frank Dawson was not a man to let nothing go by if he could account for it. Me and Dad and Ben and his dad had done work for the family many times. I did not mind Frank, he paid well and I believed he was honest. I agreed them cows was his but I did not say nothing to Daniel. You could tell by the look of them where they come from. Shorthorns, they was, big and rangy, all cock-horned and with a wild streak in them, tails up and on the lookout for trouble. They was easier scared than scrub turkeys. Daniel impounded them and I took them down to the government reserve with Mother the next day, Tip doing some quiet slipping around distracting them, keeping their minds off making a run for it, which she proved to be expert at. I seen Tip did not need no training to be an expert in stock handling and that it was in her nature, just like Irie's feelings for the ranges was in her nature. There was no rip-tear-and-bust with Tip but a quiet sneaky way of sliding around and I loved to see it. It was like she hypnotised them cows. You do not see many dogs handling cattle in the ranges as they cannot take the long miles in the heat without water. Me and Mother did not get out of a trot and them cows was in the government reserve with the bogan gate shut on them before they knew what was happening to them.

There had been no stock in the reserve paddock for months and there was plenty of fresh feed and good water in there. By the morning they had stopped walking the fence and bellowing for their freedom and was settled down to living the good life. While I was closing the bogan gate on them Tip was sitting up straight as a chair beside Mother, watching me, her tongue hanging out drooling and her eyes shining with pure pride. I told her how good I thought she was and she just about melted into the ground, grovelling around my feet and licking my boots. A dog shows gratitude for praise with a passion no other beast has in it. You cannot be impatient with a dog but have to let them get on and do their job without getting in too close on your horse, or they cannot do it so well. My dad and Ben's dad never worked with dogs and was always impatient around them and was most likely to raise their whip and give the dog's backside a sting. Them old fellers was happier when there was no dogs hanging about.

Daniel had the paperwork of it and he was doing it by the government regulations and making a big job of writing up his report on it. I think he was glad to have a real crime to report to the coast on. George Wilson would have let it work itself out and them cows would have been sold to the buyer from the meatworks the same day and the money gone to Frank, and that would have been the end of it. Them cows was no good for nothing but dog meat anyhow. I knew Ben would have dodged them from Dawsons' place for that Territorian and was most likely betting on the fellow being new to the game and not picking they was barren. Ben would not have been expecting that feller to put them in the Mount Hay yards for sale. There was not a lot of harm in it for anyone. But I seen early on I could not tell Daniel nothing and I did not try to but kept my thoughts on it to myself. He liked to have the record of everything he done in writing and filed away in that filing cabinet of his in the office and a report sent down to the police headquarters. I think all those years George Wilson was the constable there must have been dead silence from Mount Hay for the cops on the coast, and I would say they was glad to hear nothing from him. The less trouble the better would have been their philosophy.

Daniel and Esme seemed pretty much at peace with each other, and me and Irie was feeling easier about meeting up. We was taking a few more risks having our private get-togethers in the night and it got that way that I was lying awake in my clothes waiting for her to come out to my quarters for a talk pretty much every night. Miriam seen what we was up to, but Irie said she had got her sister onside and we need not worry about her. I did not ask her how she had managed that and she did not offer to tell me, but knowing Miriam I would say it was not something she would do for nothing but there must have been something in it for her. I seen Esme walking back down the track to the house from the direction of my quarters when I was riding in one day and it give me a scare to see her there. There was nothing for her once she got past the chooks and I wondered if she had been snooping around my place and getting suspicious of me and Irie meeting. It did not give me a good feeling. I did not tell Irie, as I feared she might come out with it and challenge her mother.

Me and Irie did not go out again to her shelter by the red wall but sat on my verandah to do our talking at night. That was my suggestion. Tip was always close by, her eyes blinking like she was following every word of our talk. And that's all it was. Talking was enough for me and Irie. She was pressing me to tell her when I was going to take her to the playgrounds of the Old Murri people. She wanted to see them playgrounds shining in the starlight the way I told her. The most silent place on this earth, I said. Something so still you feel the country listening to you breathe. Your horse feeling it too. And if you have a dog with you the dog will whimper and hang close to you and not go off chasing scents. I told Irie all this and she listened with a look of belief in her eyes, and I loved seeing that look and knowing myself trusted by her, and I went on with the story and made up some things that come into my head. Not lying exactly, but colouring in. I did not wish to lie outright to Irie.

There was nothing finer than being with her on my verandah telling her them things. I think I give her an idea them playgrounds was some kind of enchanted fairyland where dreams come true. Which I half believed it was myself. But not written about in her school books, or in them books of Daniel's. Them playgrounds was my own special secret that I give to her as part of us being together, just the two of us knowing it. Talking about it was our way of talking about our hopes and our own dreams and the things we was feeling about each other that we could not speak of directly. I did not expect none of it to ever be real, but I believe she did. I kept my dreams in one place and my real life in another place. But I think for Irie at that time her dreams was what she seen as her real life, and she did not separate the two. That was not something I understood then, but expected her to be like I was in everything. Which was foolish of me. She had not had her confidence dented yet. That would happen.

. . .

Rosie come around to the back door of the police house one afternoon while me and Daniel was having our smoko in the kitchen, which she knew was her time to catch the constable. She told Daniel it was Ben had branded them impounded beasts for the feller from the Territory, which everyone in town but Daniel already knew was an obvious fact. She said Ben got paid two pounds a head for them beasts. Daniel listened to her and said he would follow it up, but he did not. He had lost his trust in Rosie's word and had seen she was just after getting Ben into trouble as payback for Ben beating her boy and that is all it was with her. But we all knew it was Ben anyhow who had branded them cows. There was nothing new in that. Who else would have done it? The feller he done it for was putting a herd together out in the Territory. Ben had dodged them cows off Dawsons' place because they was barren. It stood out at you. Frank Dawson knew but he did not want Ben charged and going to gaol for it so he did not make a complaint against him. Making complaints to the police was not Frank's way of doing things and anyway he and Ben got on fine most of the time and had a lot time for each other. Frank just wanted his cows back, barren or not, or the money for the sale of them. Everyone in Mount Hay knew that except Daniel. I left it alone and said nothing.

If George Wilson had still been the constable he would not even have made no enquiries but would have left it to Frank Dawson to send a couple of his men into town to get them cows from the government reserve where I put them. When George was doing the job he would have stood up at the bar in Chiller's place and had a yarn with them men of Frank's and Ben too without making nothing of it. In George's day these things got worked out by themselves and the only time they was spoken about was if someone made some joke about them and everyone knew what they was joking about and they laughed to let the other feller know they knew what he was really talking about. An outsider like Daniel understood none of that, and even if he had understood it Esme would not have let him enjoy being an easygoing person like George Wilson was. The worst I ever seen George do was to knock the wind out of a ringer with a sharp whack in the ribs with that leather baton of his. Everyone in Mount Hay said Daniel's shirts was too starched up by his wife. I did not join in with that kind of thing. So long as I was taking the government's money I reckoned I owed Daniel something. He was my boss.

. . .

It was around my usual time for going to bed, about an hour after our evening meal. There was some thunder about up in the escarpments and the air was still and heavy with it. I was sitting on my bunk having a last smoke and looking at my mother's Bible, which I had unwrapped from her scarf and opened on my knees. I had the Bible open at the Book of Revelation, which I had heard my mother read to us many times. I knew the supper of the great God, and how we was all to eat the flesh of kings and great men and of ordinary men and I never understood it but it stayed sharp in my mind, the picture in my head of us tearing at the flesh of people to eat it. There was something so wild in that picture the truth of it stayed within me, even though I did not understand why it had to be so. I felt it in my own blood, and it stood out at times when I was troubled, as if I was told by it of the terrible things ahead. My mother told me the Book of Revelation knew my fate before I knew it myself. And I believed it in this picture of us eating the flesh of people. I do not know why. I looked at the writing but was not able to read all of it yet, my mother's beautiful soft voice in them words, holding the book open as if I might be reading it, my thoughts driven into a fantasy of a future with Irie and our kids. Which I knew was a precious dream of a fate that was not to be mine.

I was sitting on the bunk thinking these thoughts when I suddenly realised that for some time I had been hearing people shouting. It was Tip barking that woke me to it. I listened, holding my cigarette away from my mouth and not breathing to hear better. I made out it was Esme's voice and another. They was yelling at each other. I had no doubt the other voice was Irie's. I think I knew something right then at that moment. There was a chill in my guts hearing that screaming and shouting going on over at the police house.

I closed up the Bible and wrapped it in my mother's red silk scarf and put it away in the drawer and I sat and listened to the yelling coming from over at the house. I had never heard nothing like it before coming from the police house. The Collins was not much of a family for fighting with each other, not like some families in Mount Hay who was at it regularly day and night. I heard the back door slam then and I jumped. I got up off my bunk and went to the door and stepped out onto my verandah. Irie was running along the path towards me. She come up onto my verandah and she put her arms around my waist and she pressed her head against my chest. She was crying real hard, her little shoulders heaving up and down and pushing against me. I seen the door open over at the house and the shape of Daniel against the light standing looking my way. I thought, Well this is it then, Bobby Blue, and you had better be ready for it. I felt no fear but only a kind of strange calm that I always felt when something bad was happening. The calm come over me like I was not really there but was someone else watching myself, and I went very still inside. I do not think I ever had no panic in me. Even when I was cornered one time by a wild scrubber bull, I just felt cold and still and ready for it. My mother was like that too. The sky could have been falling in and she would say, Well, Bobby Blue, look what is happening to us, and she would have given me her quiet little smile. I had that from her, that calm. The light was shining out of my open door onto me and Irie clutched together there, and I knew Daniel could see us plain as day, as if we was in each other's arms. But I did not care. I was for Irie and her trouble, not for myself or for Daniel Collins.

I let her cling for a while then I reached around for her hands and I unclasped her grip on me and I held her off, being as gentle with her as I knew how to be. I said, You had better give yourself a minute to settle down, and we can sort this out. I seen Daniel's shape go back inside and the kitchen door close behind him. I cannot say why Daniel went back inside just then. If it had been Esme she would have come charging up the path and grabbed that girl and dragged her back to the house. But no doubt Esme was sitting in the kitchen recovering herself and Daniel come out to have a look. Daniel had more sense of Irie and maybe he was giving her the benefit of the doubt to sort things out herself. I cannot say for sure.

I said to Irie, You had better tell me again what you was saying. I did not follow it too plainly, Irie. She blew her nose on her hankie and wiped at her face and sniffed a couple of times. She said with a kind of violence I had not heard in her before, I hate myself for crying. I said, All women cry. There is nothing to be ashamed of in crying. She give a sad laugh at this and said, They want to send me to boarding school in town on the coast. I said, When is this going to be happening? She said, Mum's going to take me down next week to meet the school people and buy my uniforms and books. She looked at me. But I am not going, Bobby. I will run away into the scrubs. I said, It is better to make a decision when you are calm and have had time to think about it. I wondered if Daniel and Esme had started to get some feeling for how close me and Irie was getting and had decided to take her away from my influence. I did not say this, but it stood in my mind and I believe it was the case, especially Esme. Or maybe Miriam had dobbed her sister in. I will never know. Before this there had never been no talk of the Collins girls going to boarding school. The children of the big cattle stations went to boarding schools but not many of the people of the town ever sent their kids away or could afford the money to do it. The town kids just went away by themselves when they was finished with school. Some went earlier on their own and was never heard of again. Quite a few did that. Our Charley was one of them. Though I was to see Charley again one time in my life. And I will tell about that when the time is right for it.

Me and Irie stood on my verandah in the light of my doorway and we looked at each other. She was still wearing her normal day clothes. She said, I will not go back to the coast. I hate my mother. And my dad is too weak to stand up to her for me. You and me can go to the spring of the wild fig tree and live the way you were telling me the Old Murri people used to live. I said, Hold on there a second. I do not know how to live as the Old Murris lived. There is no one knows that no more. She said, We will ask Rosie. She will help us. I said, Rosie grew up in Mount Hay. She does not know a thing about living in the scrubs. Irie said, You told me you and your dad and Ben Tobin and his dad used to camp at the spring of the fig tree for days at a time. You must have found something to eat there. I said, We had our packhorses and rations, Irie. We was all geared up and ready for that kind of life. We could not have stayed too long without running out of food. Living at the spring of the old fig tree is not something anyone can do. But she was not going to be put off by my reasons. You can tell your friend Ben Tobin to bring us food, she said. She waited for me to say something to this. I said, That is not a plan that will work. She give me a long look that steadied me. You are my only friend who can help me, she said.

I did not feel too good to hear her say this. You promised to take me there one day. Now is the time to make good on that promise. She looked at me like she was suffering. I got out my tobacco and rolled a cigarette and I said again, That is not a plan that makes no sense. I can tell you that right here and now. No one has ever done nothing like that. I licked the paper down and lit the smoke and I looked at her. Only someone from the coast would come up with such a crazy idea. We will have to think of something else.

She said, When my parents see that I'm serious about this they'll give in and change their minds and let me stay. She stood checking me for a long time, no doubt wondering how she stood with me in this. They don't want me to be your friend any more, she said. That is what started me rowing with them. I told them you were better than both of them and that I love you. I said, Jesus, Irie, you said that? She said, Yes. That is what I said. And you know it is true. I told them you would take me away and we would live together in the ranges. I said, You are only just turning thirteen. Something like that cannot happen. You promised, she said. I said, I did not promise to go and live with you out in the scrub. I cannot do that. She took my hand and held it and she looked at my hand a while, then she turned up her face and looked into my eyes. She said, very quiet and solemn now, Are you on their side? I said, Hell, Irie! You know I am not on their side. She said then, in that quiet voice that upset me more than if she was screaming at me, You are going to break your promise to me. If you will not take me, then I will go on my own. Or with Miriam, if she will come along, and I think she will. I think she will be stronger in this than you are being. She let go my hand, as if she was dropping something to the ground that she was done with, and she turned around and stepped off the verandah and started walking back to the house.

I swore to myself a couple of times and called to her, Wait up, Irie! My heart was banging in my chest. She stopped and turned and looked at me, standing there on the path for all the world like a grown young woman, and I seen that is what she was, on the doorstep of her womanhood. You are not going to help me, Bobby, she said. I see I have made a mistake about you. I could think of no words to say to her that would not be a lie right at that minute.

. . .

I failed Irie that night and I know I did. I failed myself. The tragedy that was to come on us and the Collins family would not have happened if I had been stronger and had stayed staunch to Irie's dreams for us that night. Irie's strength was the second warning I had after the warning of Tip not being on the chain, but I ignored it too. She was more man than I was. I seen that and I could not deal with it right then. I just could not see how I could run off to the fig tree spring with a thirteen-year-old girl who was the constable's daughter. It did not make no sense to me at all. Ben might have done it one time, but I was not wild enough for something like that and I never had been. If I took her out to Ben's place he would think of something. I knew that. But I knew I was not going to do that neither. Getting her mixed up with Ben as a runaway was not my idea of how this should go for her or for me. I seen she was something like Ben herself and was ready to take things as far as she wished them to go and make nothing of the law and how people would think of her. Like Ben, she was her own boss in a way I never was.

She stood on the path waiting for me to speak, it seemed like forever. The thunder was turning over in the black sky and I could smell rain in the air. I felt a deep sadness when I finally said, One day when you have your freedom you will be able to come back out here. I will still be here. I am not going nowhere. In three or four years time you will have your freedom from school and from your parents and you can choose to do as you please then and no one will be able to stop you. I hear myself saying these things now and I know how sad and weak I must have sounded to her and to myself, the dreams and storytelling gone out of my voice altogether. I heard it. She said in that calm sad way that she was accusing me with, It will not be three or four years, Bobby, but eight years before I am twenty-one and am free. Till then they can stop me, and they will if I let them. I am not waiting till I am twenty-one. She had lost the hope of my help and I had no answer for her. I said, I do not see another way for you, Irie. She said in that voice she had, No, you do not see another way for me, Bobby, and you see no way at all for us. I would stay with you if you did see a way. I felt at that moment that she was somehow older and wiser than I was then or would ever be in my entire life and I could not meet her at her level. I felt sick to know it.

Daniel come out at the kitchen door and stood in the light looking our way. He called to her, his call sudden. Irie! Just that.

Her name. I felt a strangeness go through me hearing her father's sharp cry of her name called into the night. He was finished with waiting. Like it was the last time he would ever call his child to him. I felt it and it give me a shiver to hear it and I wondered what it meant for all of us and I wished my mother had been there to tell me the right way of this. The thunder rolled and tumbled in the sky and Irie turned away from me and walked on down the path towards the house and her father, her name sounding in my head. Irie! Sharp, like a cry that was to go on sounding forever after, falling away only in years to come, fading into some great distance I could not imagine, until it was lost in time to me and her both. I watched her until the back door closed on her, and then I stood, not seeing the door but seeing her and seeing something in myself, something proved about myself that I had not known before, something tested and failed, a fear I had no understanding of at the time. But I knew myself to be less of a free man than I had believed I was. I knew that in my place Ben would not have let her go like that but would have taken her out into the scrub and made a run for it, no matter what. And I knew he would have been right to do that. But still I did not do it. I stood knowing I had betrayed her. The best thing that ever come into my life. Irie Collins. Her mark was never to leave me.

. . .

I stood a while then stepped off the verandah and walked down to the horse paddock and climbed through the wire and went on to the back fence and climbed through and walked on into the scrub. The lightning cracked and flashed and I looked back and seen the horses lit up, galloping the fence like silent creatures that was strange to me. I kept going until I got to Irie's camp. I did not go in the shelter but lay on my back on the ground litter. I looked up into the storming sky, and there was nothing I knew there, the lightning tearing this way and that, the great clouds like a rolling flood torn by the storm winds, the brigalow sticks clacking and chattering in the violent wind like mad women determined on some savagery. I knew myself to be looking into the sea of glass mingled with fire of Revelation, when the world will come apart and we will all burn. A splash of rain hit my face and I heard it coming above the thunder, thrashing through the timber like a crazed old scrubber bull. The rain come down out of the sky like God had decided to wash us all clean of our sins before he burned us to cinders as was promised in the last days for all of us sinners. I lay in the rain waiting to drown or sink into the earth and be forgotten like them Old People was forgotten. I was filled with terror and was despised and found nothing familiar to comfort me, but all was strange about me and was heavy on me with an evil that was a rancid smell in my throat.

. . .

It was breaking day when I woke. The sky was clear, the last of the stars winking out. I got up and walked back to my quarters. I felt nothing but shame. I could not make a cigarette. My tobacco and papers was soaked through and was no use to me. I lay on my bunk in my wet clothes and went to sleep. I did not wake up for some hours. They was all finished eating their breakfasts when I got over to the police house. Esme was not in the kitchen but I seen my breakfast plate sitting on a saucepan with the lid over my eggs and corned beef. The water in the saucepan had gone cold. I felt strange to be there, and knew I should always have felt strange in the police house and should never have tried to make it my home but should have followed my instincts on it. There was a sickness in me I could not deal with. While I was eating my cold eggs Daniel come into the kitchen. He asked me to step around to the office and see him after I was finished and he went out again.

When I come into the office he was sitting behind his desk, his shirt all fresh starched, his hands on the desk fiddling with his pen and the papers that was there. Esme was sitting off to one side of him, her lips tight and her eyes hard and narrowed. It looked like I was to have a police interview. Daniel said, Thank you for coming in, Bobby. As if he thought there was a chance I might not have come in. Mrs Collins has something to say to you, he said. I looked at Esme.

Irie's mother was looking at me like she wanted to see me hung from that old dead lemon tree which she hated so much. She was breathing deep, her breasts swelling up and down under her stripy dress. She met my eyes and we looked at each other. She spoke at me through her lips, without screaming or nothing, but holding it in. To think I made you welcome in our home, she said. She twisted her lips around with disgust when she spoke. I wondered how long she was going to keep from giving it to me full throttle. We gave you our trust! she said. Our trust! And this is the way you have repaid us. She sat in silence for some time, breathing and looking at me like I was a worm she had found in her cereal. I thought of us sitting together and me reading to her. I heard Fay's Blitz going by and I listened for it to change down as she hit into the hill. Fay must have had a big load on because she changed down before the motor begun to strain at the hill. I was wondering what was on that load. Esme leaned forward and she looked right into my eyes and said, like each word was a little river stone, I want you to know how much I despise you for this. That is all I have to say to you. She straightened up and looked at

Daniel, like she was telling him it was his turn now and to get on with finishing it. Daniel cleared his throat a couple of times. Do you have anything to say to Mrs Collins, Bobby? He frowned at me like he was trying to remind me that I had forgotten something and needed to say it.

But I could not think of nothing to say so I said nothing. It did not seem right to me that Esme had judged me before I had a chance to tell her the way I seen things and how it stood for me. I was not Irie, I was me. Daniel letting Esme have her say like that, insulting me before they give me a chance to speak, was not a good way of going about this. It put me down from the word go and I sat there knowing myself to be a judged man, and found guilty. My guilt, which I did feel with a great heaviness, was not for them to know but was private to me, and was the guilt of betraying their daughter's trust in me and was not for nothing else. I had a mind to get up and walk out. I seen whatever I said they was not going to change their minds about me. I was thinking they could go to hell with their questions and I did not defend myself to them. It was a mistake to say nothing but I did not know that until later. I was thinking maybe if I went down to the school I could find Irie and tell her to come on with me to the spring of the old fig tree, and somehow we would make a go of it or perish together out in the scrubs trying. But I sat on there, facing them two, waiting for what else they had in mind for me. I did not believe I had done nothing criminal and was not expecting Daniel to charge me, but I seen he was not done with me yet. I had nothing to fear from them. Their judging of me made me angry and I seen the flames of that fire in my dream again and me snatching Irie from the flames and looking back to watch them all burning, that great fire wind howling and moaning around them. The flames of hell. That is what it was. The flames from that last book in my mother's Bible that she read to me and Dad so many times over the years, her love of the sacred words of it and their mystery. What she always called the last word. I remembered those words always: His eyes were as a flame of fire and he was clothed in blood. I laughed and Esme turned to Daniel and said, You see? You see? I told you there was no point giving this creature the benefit of the doubt. Creature I was. I heard her say it.

Daniel half closed his eyes. I seen how uncomfortable he was and I pitied him for it. He kind of nodded his head and breathed and shifted himself on his chair so it squeaked, as if his backside was getting sore sitting there. I said, I will be down the shed when you need me, and I stood up. Daniel said, Just a minute, Bobby. Sit down! I have something to say to you myself. I did not sit down but stood where I was. I said, If you have something to say to me you can say it down the shed. That is where I will be.

He stood and shouted at me, Just sit down! And listen to me! I looked at him, to see him losing his control like this, and I felt superior to him. I decided to go and get Irie and make a run for it. I said, You should listen to your own mind, not the mind of your wife. She stood up and said, I will leave you to it, and she come around the desk and was careful to avoid touching me and she went out the door behind me. Daniel said, Please, Bobby! Will you sit down. I sat down. He said, Thank you. I said, You have judged me. Daniel said, It's over. There's nothing to say. We can't have you in the house. He looked at me a while. I hope you understand that. What will you do? I laughed. He said, I am very sorry this has happened. I could see he was expecting me to say something, maybe to try to excuse myself to him or get him to see things my way, but I would not say nothing to him. I might have told him that wife of his would get him killed one of these days, but I kept that thought to myself too. My dad would not have stayed so long with these people as I had stayed with them.

I wondered if my dad would have taken Irie with him if he was in my situation and gone off somewhere with her without saying nothing to no one. I could see him doing it and I believe he would have. My dad never asked no one's permission to live the way he lived and he never went to the police to settle his problems but settled them his own way. Daniel said, You can sleep in the quarters tonight but I will expect you to be gone in the morning. You can get your dinner at the hotel. I will pay Chiller for your dinner and I will pay you what you are owed in wages. Sitting there looking at Constable Daniel Collins I could see Ben laughing when I told him this story. Ben would be telling me what a damn fool I had been to ever think I could work for the police. I smiled, for I had suddenly seen what my decision was to be. I would saddle Mother first thing in the morning and meet Irie on her way to school and take her out to Ben's place. I could already feel her sitting up behind me on Mother, her arms around my waist and her head pressed into my back. I would tell her I was sorry for my weakness and she would believe in me again. She and Deeds would get on fine. Deeds would look after her. We could decide what to do after we got there. Ben would have an idea. We would be our own family.

My strength come back in me as soon as I had this decision in my mind. My mother would see how I redeemed myself by this not only in Irie's eyes but in my own. I was set on it. I stood up. You don't owe me nothing, I said. Chiller will feed me without requiring payment from you. I looked at him steady, calculating what I might say to him. You have not understood us people of the ranges, I said. Chiller knew my dad and me all our lives. You don't need to pay Chiller nothing for my tucker. I turned around and went out and walked around to the hotel and got myself tobacco and papers. It was a good feeling to be a free man again. I would take her away with me like she asked me to. I seen how I had been losing belief in myself for a long time working with them coast people at the police house. I was glad to be done with them. I had no fear of what was to happen. I would be accused of kidnapping their child, but I did not care. Me and Irie would find a way for ourselves. We had our whole lives to see to it.

TEN

That final night on my bunk in the two-man quarters I thought I was dreaming a horse was standing on my chest. I tried to push it off but could not and I opened my eyes. It was already getting light, cockatoos screeching, the chooks going crazy like they had a fox in the pen with them. I opened my eyes. Daniel was leaning over me, pressing down with his open hand up close to my throat so I could hardly breathe. I was gripping his wrist with my own hand. He had his face bent close to mine. I could smell his breath, like there was something sour in him. The girls are gone, he said, kind of panting the words out, that sour breath in my face, saying his words and taking a gasp of air like he had been running hard to reach me. I tried to sit up but he pressed down heavy, holding me there. I seen in his eyes he was not the mild man I had made him out to be but was changed. Where are they, Bobby? There was nothing but menace in his use of my name. His spittle hit my eye and I blinked and snapped my head to one side. I seen he was gripping that leather baton of George's in his free hand and meant to use it on me right then if I did not give him the answer he was looking for pretty smartly. I said, You can ease up. I know where they have gone to. He stepped away and let me up. Get your gear on! He spoke to me like I was already his prisoner and of no account to him as a man.

I slipped out of my bunk and dragged my clothes on. He stood back, his eyes going around my quarters with suspicion then swinging back to me. Oh yeah, you know where they are, he said. He was wearing his fresh ironed uniform as usual, the Webley .38 on his belt alongside that pouch with the handcuffs in it. He was without his hat. His voice was low and thick with some emotion when he said to me, If anything has happened to my girls I will kill you. It stilled something in me to hear him say it. His voice was like he was speaking of the end of his own life. That is how I felt it. As if he was seeing his own death and mine and everything for him was now changed and a new time was come upon him, the old time and its dreams fallen behind him, broken and lost in the drift. Things to say to him come into my mind but I did not consider it a good time to say them, so I kept quiet. I saw a movement and suddenly realised it was his wife standing in the doorway behind him, a kind of dark shadow out there in the cold light of the morning. I had not heard Esme come up to the quarters.

Daniel said, He knows where they are. In my hurry to get my pants on I tripped and sat down hard on the edge of my bunk, hurting my backside. Esme did not say nothing but stood looking in at me as if I was a beast they had cornered. She was wearing an apron over her dress and her hair was free and wild and hanging loose about her head. She did not look like the neat Mrs Esme Collins I was used to seeing.

I had my head down pulling my boots on, sitting on the side of my bunk. Daniel grabbed me by the back of my neck and he forced my head hard between my knees and he put the cuffs on my wrists behind my back. He dragged me up and pushed me out the door ahead of him. Esme stepped back and stared at me. I stumbled off the verandah ahead of them. The early morning air was cool and fresh and light against my skin, a perfume of wattle flowers on the breeze. My head felt naked without my hat but I could see there was to be no going back for it. Mother was at the horse paddock fence looking over at us, her ears pricked up. When she seen me stumbling ahead of Daniel and his missus she give out a snort and tossed her head, trotting stiffly up along the fence then back again, just as if she had seen a big old king brown snake over this way. Mother hated them old brown snakes more than anything. It was plain enough she did not like the look of what she was seeing. Daniel give me a shove in the back and I seen Tip sneaking along beside us low in the grass, her ears flat against her skull and her hindquarters hunched down and dragging. I never seen a dog look more disheartened.

Daniel stood me on the path and he said, Where are they? I believe he would have shot me there if he had not needed me so badly just then. I seen in his eyes it was what he wanted to do. I said, There is no need for these cuffs. I will not be running off nowhere. He hauled back and whacked me hard in the ribs with that leather baton. The air come out of me and I made a noise and felt my knees give. He hauled me up and put his mouth close to my ear. Where are they? He spoke like he might choke on his words. I shook my head to clear it and sucked in air. They will be at their cubby house out in the bendee, I said. I will take you there. Too right you will, he said and he give me a crack across the back of my head with his open palm. I said, There is no need to go beating on me, Mr Collins. I am taking you there. He give me another good hard whack with his hand and I tripped and nearly went down. He hauled me up and pushed me forward. I reckoned if I was wrong about where the girls was then my chances was going to be thin with these two, for I seen there was a kind of panic and fear had got hold of them in their need to see their girls safe. I could have told them Irie and Miriam was fine but there was no way they was going to listen to me. Them two had a fear of the scrubs. A fear of their own ignorance. I could have told them their girls was safer in the scrubs than they ever was in the town. I had never worn cuffs before and had not realised how thrown from his balance a man is with his hands manacled behind his back. I knew myself wide open to whatever come at me without no defence of it. It was not a good feeling to be made so helpless.

Tip stopped at the fence and stood making a whining sound, watching us go like she was never to see us again but was too afraid to come with us. Whatever it was holding her back, dogs know things we cannot know. I did not feel easy seeing Tip hanging back like that. We went through the horse paddock, the horses spooked like crazy, and I thought one of them might go clean through the wire and injure itself. I called out to Mother to steady her but she had the fear in her just like the others. She come up close then ducked and kicked off and screwed to a sliding stop at the wire, her hind legs going under her and her rump hitting the ground with a thud. I seen her throw her head back, her eye white with the fear, and I felt a touch of her despair in my own guts. A horse will wind things and you cannot fool them with what is going on like you can fool cattle. If I had known then that I had ridden her for the last time I would have sat down on the ground and wept and refused to go another inch, and Daniel could have beat me with that baton of his all he pleased and I would not have moved for him. But I did not know that, just as we never know the last time for nothing, either to weep or to eat our last meal. The last time had come and gone for me and that mare, and I never knew nothing of it but kept going across that morning paddock as if the two of us was to ride out again together, free and content in the scrubs we both loved to be in.

I seen Rosie then. She was standing still as a dead tree over next to the shed, watching us. It give me a shock to see that dark woman standing there and I did not know what to make of it, but I knew it was not a good sign for me. Them Old Murris have the gift to read the signs. But us whitefellers do not have that gift to read the future in the signs we see today, but only when we look back do we see how we might have read them. If we had that gift our lives would not go as they do but would go in other ways. My mother told me many times, giving me that sweet smile of hers and touching my hair lovingly with her hand, We go forward into the dark, Bobby Blue, knowing nothing of our fate but putting our trust in the Lord Jesus Christ who is our Saviour. That is how my mother lived. Her faith was steady. But mine faltered. I have seen how a man is alive one minute and dead the next without knowing nothing of it. That is the way it happens for us. As it does for the beasts. We see nothing of it till it is on us. I did not wish to be affected by that fierce panic that was in Daniel and Esme but I felt it around me, just as the horses felt it. It was like a sickness without a cure and I knew I could not stay clean of it. I was only a man myself and had no special powers. I knew that. I felt it. My hands held by them steel rings behind my back felt it. What are we without our hands? We are as the beasts. And without faith that is all we are. As the beasts. I knew it in my soul as I walked on, leading them two despairing parents into the morning, my stomach empty with the knowing of my own weakness.

At the far side of the horse paddock Daniel put his foot on the bottom wire and lifted the middle strand for me to climb through. As I bent down to get through I thought of holding the wire for Irie. The back of my shirt caught on the barb and when I made to look around to get myself unhooked Daniel pushed me through with his boot so I landed on my face. My police shirt tore and I felt the stab of the barb going in my flesh. I found it is not so easy to get up from a lying-down position without the use of your hands and arms and I scrabbled around trying to get my feet under me like an emu hit by a motor along the road. I seen them emus scrabble around just like I was doing. When Daniel and Esme was through the fence Daniel dragged me to my feet and pushed me forward. I heard him curse a couple of times. Esme said nothing. Not one word come out of that woman's mouth, just that staring panicky fear in her eyes. I do not think she knew what she was going to do and had no control of what she might decide on. I seen her actions was just going to come out of her suddenly and take her off-guard. There was no reasoning with that look she had, and she did not belong to herself but belonged to her fear. Her dream was to be rid of me and to have her girls back safe in her arms, laughing and weeping and hugging them to herself and forgiving them for putting her under the biggest scare of her life.

. . .

We went on into the scrub and I headed for the red outcrop. I started thinking these two would owe me an apology when we got there and found the girls having their picnic of biscuits and dates in that humpy Irie and Miriam had made. I thought of me and Irie sitting cross-legged in there that night, talking by the light of the candle about our dreams, and how I would have done everything I could to make sure no harm ever come to that girl. Give my life if it was asked of me. The injustice burned in me. That picture of how this was to turn out was the best I could hope for. But I knew there was something not right about it. I could feel the wrongness of it, circling us, circling all of us, me and Ben and Deeds and Irie and everyone. A feeling of being encircled by it, so we was all dizzy and not seeing straight and going in circles like people who is lost in the bush go in circles, crossing their own tracks again and again until they are out of time. My dream of our little family together with Deeds and Ben and their kid was lost to me in the dizziness of this.

Like her mother and father, Irie had changed too. I had witnessed her finding the edge of her grown-up world the other night and being called by the touch of it to go on with it and hunt after it. That screaming and yelling with her mother had brought out the determined hunger in her to be free of them and to be herself. I seen it before. It was no different with beasts. Once they kick and feel the power of striking home, they go on kicking till they is either dead or has struggled to their freedom. It was natural. I seen it with Ben when he got sick of his dad beating on him and run off to the coast and worked in the Townsville meatworks that time. Ben was not much older then than Irie was now. When he come back into the ranges Ben was his own man and except for that one last time his dad never beat him again but learned to know him as a man equal to himself. There was no difference in this with Irie wanting to be free of her mother. All creatures struggle for their freedom from the nest. It is the way we are. Who does not do it?

A young owl will risk its life to fly that first time. I have seen it. They will hiss at you with their last breath when they are grounded.

I seen a big old-man roo at the edge of a stand of brigalow watching us coming through. When we got close he did not turn and head out but stood tall and give a bit of a cough to us. That roo made me think of Rosie standing back there like a shadow at the corner of the shed, knowing something us three did not know, knowing the way of the dizzying circle we was in. That was her. My dad called her the Black Rose. Dad was polite to everyone he ever met as a fellow human being but I noticed as a boy he was always extra polite with Rosie and would lift his hat when he come on her. I believe he had some fear of her and her knowledge. The roo was hot for something and was not getting out of our way. Daniel and Esme did not see him. They seen nothing but the picture of their two girls in their minds, Daniel urging me along as if I was a piker bullock and was stubborn to go. But I was not stubborn, just hindered by having my hands behind my back. Esme alongside in her dress and shoes, stumbling and silent. She might as well have had her eyes closed. I do not think Esme had ever been into the scrubs before, but I believe that morning she would have stepped into the fires of hell without feeling their heat to get her girls back. I thought there might be a wild dog around holding the roo up, but I seen no tracks of one.

As soon as we come out of the bendee onto a piece of open ground the girls' tracks was clear as day in the whiteness of the clay. There was no shade and the sun was already hot on my head without my hat, which I was not used to. I pulled up and said, See! Here's where they come through. With the cuffs on I could not point properly and Daniel did not know what I was telling him. Irie and Miriam's tracks, I said. Here! Take a look. Him and Esme looked hard at the ground like they expected to see their daughters come floating up out of the earth. Watching the pair of them it seemed to me I was in the power of two dangerous people. I put a calmness in my voice and said, They was walking side by side. Most likely holding hands if you ask me. They will be out there in that cubby house of theirs eating biscuits and dates and making their plans. Them two looked at me like I was speaking a foreign language to them. I tried a smile but I do not think it worked too well on them.

You would not think I would laugh at such a moment but that is what I did right then. It just come out of me when I seen them two puzzling at me then peering at the tracks then looking at each other. It was not much of a laugh but was more a nervous kind of giggle on account of my relief at seeing the girls' tracks, which I had been searching for, knowing that if I did not see them I was in real trouble. Daniel must have thought I was mocking them.

When I laughed he swung around and hit me hard in the face with that police baton of his. It was a reaction that just come to him with all the tension that was in him. I seen that. He did not give it no thought. He was so tight with his panic to see his girls alive and well and was blaming me for his fear. I was not looking for it and the blow caught me full across the bridge of my nose. I sat down on my backside, my right hand bending under me and nearly breaking my wrist, the iron edges of the manacles cutting into my flesh. I give a yelp of pain and Daniel grabbed my shirt and dragged me onto my feet. His face had gone a dark mottled red in the sunlight, strange white patches under his eyes. The birds was going wild around us, a whole tribe of black crows dive-bombing the bendee over our heads like we was trespassing on their ground and stirring up their Old People.

I felt suddenly very low at that moment and seemed to know in my heart this thing was not going to work out well for me. I still had my picture of the girls in their cubby house, and I clung to it, but I knew it was not a picture of anything real. In my own way I seen I was just as lost with this thing as Esme and Daniel was. We was three fools trampling around in the scrubs, blind to good sense and to the certainty of our own fate. Which is what my mother would have said. We are blind to our own fate, that is what she always said.

When we come on Irie's shelter I seen at once the girls was not there. My guts sank and there was an emptiness in me. By the look of their tracks they had not even stopped but had gone straight past. I reckoned Irie was making for the red wall and the playgrounds of the Old Murri people, which I had made her see as some kind of magic place. Her direction was off by a couple of degrees. A couple of degrees in the scrubs is the difference between getting where you want to go and getting somewhere else entirely. There is no point taking the wrong line in the scrubs unless you want to get yourself lost. Daniel got down on his knees and looked into the entrance of the shelter, Esme getting down and looking in over his shoulder, her hand to his back. As if they was hoping to find their two girls hidden in some dark corner, giggling and just playing an innocent old game of hidey after all. Daniel's voice come out hollow from the cubby house: They are not here. The pair of them stayed down looking in at the emptiness, hoping I suppose where there was no hope to be had. Esme said, So that is where those dates went. She almost sounded normal when she said this and it give me a gentle feeling towards her to hear her speaking just like my own mother would have spoken at that moment. So that is where those dates went. As if knowing how come she lost the dates was the biggest satisfaction for her just then.

Daniel crawled out and stood up and looked at Esme. She got up and put her hands to her mouth and called, I . . . reee! Mi . . . reee! She listened then turned a half pace, facing more to the south, and called again, her voice waking the crows and sending a flock of feeding cockatoos flapping and screeching out of the brigalow sticks. We stood waiting to hear Irie's voice coming back to us out of the silence. But it was just Esme's voice come back to us, faint and empty and filled with the quiet of the bush, like a ghost calling to us from the escarpments, mocking our hopes. Esme stood and called their names and called again and again, then suddenly she bent double and began to cry, making loud sobbing noises like she had been overcome with a sudden horror of it. Daniel put his hand to her back and stood close beside her, helpless to know what to do.

I felt sorry for them two. I wished in my heart none of this had happened to them. But there was also a stranger in me I had not known before that morning. He stood by and looked on at this scene in the scrubs without no feelings for it, but as if he knew it was always meant to be this way and there was nothing none of us could ever have done different to change the way it was. It was the first time I met that stranger and I did not like to know him. I have met him many times since that day and he has become a familiar to me. I seen we three was sharing something that morning that we did not understand, and maybe never would understand, something bigger than each of us. I have had time to think about it over and over again, and I still do not understand it. It resists me and is like a door closed against my thoughts.

. . .

Common sense told me the girls was up ahead of us, somewhere between where we was standing and maybe a mile or so off to the south of the playgrounds, depending on the head start they had on us. I was wondering if Irie packed the two of them up and got away in the night. Or had she waited till it was coming on to dawn before heading out? Again Tip had not alerted no one to them two leaving, which she would have done if she had been on the chain. Being off the chain she probably went along with them some way for the adventure of it until Irie told her to get home. I was not a good enough tracker to pick the time of their passing from the signs they had left in the claypan. They could be miles ahead or just over the near rise. My dad would have known. My dad could track a moth through the scrubs on a moonless night. He had a feel for it I never did have. It was the feel for it he followed, not the sign on the ground. You cannot teach tracking, it is like the voice of a singer. It has to be in you if it is to come out of you.

The ground was a series of undulations and small shallow valleys all running into each other, and we only got a general view of the country every once in a while when we was on top of a rise and found a clear line through the dense scrub. On foot we saw very little. If you are on a horse you see more. I had never been through there on foot in my whole life. On foot we was down in among the thick of things and it was not possible to see more than fifty yards ahead of ourselves at the best of it, and a lot less most of the time. It was ideal country for wild scrubber cattle and I knew it like I knew my own self, even on foot. Them scrubs was home to me since I was old enough to run off after school, and I did not need to bother thinking about where I was to know where I was. I just knew where I was. I was thinking of Irie going along with her fine courage, holding Miriam's hand and telling her about the magic of the playgrounds and giving her hope of the adventure of getting to the spring of the old fig tree, even though she would have had little idea herself how she might ever get to that place. That fig tree was a good two days ride from the playgrounds. I looked at Daniel and Esme and they seemed to have forgotten about me. I said, Irie is trying to get to the playgrounds of the Old Murri people. Them playgrounds is a long way off from here. We should turn around and come back on horses. There is no water between here and Coal Creek. We will need to bring water for the girls. And we should get our hats too or we will soon cook.

Them two turned around and looked at me. Sweat was staining Daniel's clean ironed shirt and Esme's dress was clinging to her and she was plucking at it under her arms to free the material from her skin. They was hot and flushed and wild in their eyes, as if they had fallen into a trap and did not know the way out of it. We stood in our own silence a while, the bird sounds giving us the feel of space and emptiness that I loved to feel around me but which must have made them two feel they was lost to all the usual things of their life. I could feel my heart pumping my blood around in my body and I thought to myself how fit and well I was and how much life there was still in me. I had my whole strength and had never had a day's illness in my entire life. I was wishing I was sitting up on Mother instead of standing in my boots without my hat with my hands gripped in them iron rings behind my back.

My eyes was on Daniel's eyes and his eyes stayed on mine and we both waited for something. I do not know what it was we was waiting for, but it held us like we was in a room alone together sworn to silence until the word was given for us to speak. I seen I would have to say something. I said, Irie has tried to make it to the playgrounds of the Old Murri people but she has not gone in the exact right direction.

Daniel kind of woke up and wiped at his face with his open hand and looked at his hand. He then looked at me. What did you say? I repeated myself again. He and Esme looked defeated with the horror of the thoughts of their girls that was in them. I said I had told Irie stories of the playgrounds and they puzzled at me to hear me saying it. I seen the hope of their girls struggling in them against their terror of loss and death. And I seen the disgust they had of being forced to listen to me on the subject of their daughters. I do not know what they had in their minds about what me and Irie might have got up to, but I do know it was not good. They had not trusted their daughter no more than they had trusted me. They did not know the kind of man I was or they would have had no fear of Irie being my friend. And I believe they did not know their daughter neither, but only had fear in themselves for her. I said, We had better go back and get the horses. And the sooner the better. The girls will be out there somewhere and it is rough country for walking in and it gets a lot rougher from here on. And it is only going to get hotter as we follow the watershed.

Daniel said, What watershed? Like he thought there was a secret in what I was saying and I was leading him on, his confused mind suspicious of some deeper trap he might be walking into, his girls, his wife and himself all swallowed up out there in that poison bendee scrub. I said, You do not see it because it is only gradual, but we have crossed over onto the Coal Creek side and the land declines down from here. He looked around. That ridge, he said, suspicion loud in his voice and pointing, is higher than this ground. I said, It is, but the way of the country is down from here generally till you get to Coal Creek. After Coal it rises again onto the western side till it peaks at the Dixon Creek watershed. I could have given him a detailed description of the map of the country east of Mount Hay that I had in my head but it would just have confused him further. He stared hard at me and wiped at his face with that downward sweep of his hand again. He was a man suffering. He turned to Esme. Maybe we should do as he says, he said. Esme give him a sick look. You can go back if you want to, Daniel Collins, she said. I am going on until I find my girls. Daniel said, There is no need for you to take that tone with me, Ez. We are in this together. But if there is no water we will all be in trouble soon enough. He is right about that. I do not like to listen to him any more than you do, but what he says is true.

Then it was suddenly like someone had lit a match to dry grass in a wind and they was flaring up with all the fear and tension coming out of them in a rush of hatred for each other. She swung around on him and shouted in his face, Are you happy now? Are you satisfied with your stupid adventure in the ranges? You brought us up here, Daniel Collins, and look where it has got us! He come back at her, It was you invited him to eat in the house with the girls. That was not my idea. And just look what that has brought us to. She slapped him hard across the face and he reeled back and snatched at her wrist and held her, the sting of her blow making his eyes water and setting his hat sideways on his head. I thought he was going to hit her but he held off. She struggled against his grip on her wrist and cried out at him, and he held her a while, showing her he was stronger and she could not break his grip till he wanted to let her go. She shouted at him, You are the stupidest man I ever met! I hate you! These people have been laughing at you ever since the day we arrived.

He let her go with a flinging of his hand and she fell back against the shelter. He was yelling at her that she had been a willing partner coming into the ranges and more the cause of their troubles than he was. You want to control every damn thing and you have no idea of the damage you do to people. If you had not insisted Irie go to boarding school but had kept your calm and listened to her none of this would have happened. I thought he had a good point with this, but Esme was past hearing him. I seen the thought of murder in the wildness of her eyes. I do not remember all the exact things they accused each other of, but it was like they suddenly hated each other more even than the fear of losing their girls. Then Esme was heading off on her own. Daniel shouted to her to come back but she went on. I said, She will not be able to follow them tracks once they go into the scrub again. She will not see nothing of them once she gets into the bendee, there is too much ground litter. Daniel turned around and he looked at me. Nothing would give me more satisfaction than to shoot you right here and now where you stand, he said.

He turned around and called to Esme that he was coming and for her to wait up but she kept going. He undid the buckle on his Webley and he pulled that gun out and fired a shot into the air. I thought, I am next. At the sound of the shot echoing around the scrub Esme stopped and turned around and looked back at us. He give me a hard push in the back and said, Get going. Esme stood and waited and I went past her and led them across the open claypan and into the bendee again. I had a feeling I was walking to my own death.

. . .

I soon lost Irie's and Miriam's tracks among the ground litter but I had a good feel for their direction and I followed the natural run of the country, keeping not too far south of the red wall, which I could see from time to time over on our left, unless we was down in a gully. It was the natural way a stranger would go. I knew where there was a number of rock pools that would have water in them after the storms and I was hoping Irie would come on them. I did not see their tracks again but kept going anyhow, hoping I was going to cross them sooner or later. A person who is lost will tend to work their way around in a circle until they cross their own tracks, which Chiller told me once was something to do with the way the earth was turning around. I am not sure of that. But I always thought there might be something in it. Chiller knew things I did not know.

The bendee is low and dense and does not give a lot of shade. The country over that way soon gets uneven with rocky outcrops. The sun was hot on my head, my back burning where my shirt was torn open from the barb. We went on in silence, the three of us. I was dry in the throat but I believe they must have been a lot drier in their throats than I was in mine from all their yelling at each other. And I had gone without water plenty of times for a whole day. Neither of them said nothing, but just walked along behind me. I did not look around to see how they was going. I was wondering if Daniel had put that revolver back in its holster or was maybe still carrying it with the idea of using it at some stage. It give me a tight feeling in my back thinking of him coming on behind me with that gun in his hand. Daniel Collins was always a lost man in the scrub. I had not had no breakfast and kept thinking of a drink of tea and a couple of fried eggs. With death maybe an inch away I could still think of my stomach. But I loved to eat in them days.

Halfway through the morning I seen something blue over to our left and I stopped and turned around to them. I said, There is something over there they dropped. I was glad to see Daniel had holstered the gun. Him and Esme went over and took up the thing. They come back and Daniel said, They can't be far away. He put his hands around his mouth and yelled Irie's name and we waited. There was no echo from where we was but I seen a black hawk rise and peel away. Daniel's call fell dead among the stand of brigalow we had got into. Him and Esme looked at each other. He reached and touched her arm and said, I'm sorry for what I said. She nodded to him and did not look up from the blue handkerchief. She did not apologise back to him. I had seen wild pig rootings and I reckoned there would be water not too far off.

I went on and they followed behind me, Esme first and him coming on last, the scrape and crackle of their footsteps through the litter. I cut across a low ridge to get out of the brigalow and the ground fell away sharply into a steep gully. I did not know how I would go with my hands behind my back and I asked Daniel if he would loose the cuffs till I had made my way down the steep. He said, We do not have to go down there. We can go across lower, and he pointed along where it was not so steep. I said, This is the only place where they will have found water. You might like to get a drink yourself. I seen he was hesitating whether to take the cuffs off me. Esme said, If you turn him loose he will run off and leave us to our fate out here or you will have to shoot him. Which will be the same thing. It has been his plan all along. Can't you see that? Him and that Ben Tobin have had their plan to get back at you and you are too simple and trusting to see it. Daniel did not say nothing to this but he frowned hard with what was going through his thoughts.

I said, I never had no plan, Mrs Collins. She screamed at me, Shut up! Shut up! She screamed it three times and nearly choked herself trying to scream it a fourth time. She was clutching on to that blue hankie and her face was bright red, her dress all sweated up and nicked here and there with branches that had dragged at her. I said, I will get down the best way I can. We will not get ourselves a drink nowhere else out this way. I got down on my backside and worked my way down into the bottom of the gully. I felt just like a broken-backed dog dragging its arse. I was glad my dad could not see me.

The pools of water were cupped in the narrow bottom among the tumbled rock. The pigs had not been down there. The pools was small and filled with no more than a billy of water each. The water was clear and I seen at once the girls had not been there. If they had drunk at any of these little places the water would have been clouded with being stirred up. I stood back and watched

Esme and Daniel get down on their bellies and suck up a drink. He had left the Webley's holster flap unbuckled and I thought I could have sat on him and hauled that gun out and had the better of the pair of them. But I looked ahead of doing it and seen there was nowhere for me to take it from there without committing some terrible crime and destroying my life and theirs forever after. And that was not something I could seriously think about doing. It made my heart race standing there looking down at him thinking about doing it all the same. I was still thinking about the whack he give me with that leather baton of his. When it was my turn to get a drink he held me by the shirt and helped me squirm myself into position. There was only a cup of water left and it was all stirred up and murky. I had drunk a lot worse many times and been more hard-pressed for it than I was just then, but I had never drunk on my belly in the bottom of a gully with cuffs on. That was something new for me.

. . .

It was late in the day and we was all pretty well done up when we come on the rock shelter and seen the girls had been there a few hours ahead of us. There was a scuffed-up sandy patch out the front of the rock shelter. The three of us stood out the front and Daniel said to me, Do you think they have been here? The first thing I seen among all that scuffing was the fresh tracks of two unshod horses. I did not stop to think about what I was saying but was so relieved to see this sight I just come out with it. I said, Ben and Deeds have picked them up. They are okay. Ben and Deeds would have come through this way from visiting in Mount Hay on their way home to Coal Creek. It looks like the girls had themselves a little fire going. I was full of admiration for Irie getting a fire going with the ground litter dull from the storms. It looked like that girl was a long way from feeling lost and panicked. I wished to tell this to her mother and father so that they might admire her too, but I was not fool enough to try doing it just then. I would like to have bragged about her to them.

Esme took Daniel off a little way and was whispering something to him, the pair of them looking across at me with suspicion. Daniel come over to me and stood in front of me and he suddenly drew back his arm and cracked me one across the side of my head with his fist. I went over backwards and sat down hard on my backside. He crouched down in front of me and hauled that Webley out of its holster and stuck it in my face. Now you will tell me this plan of yours with Ben Tobin to get his revenge on me or I will finish you right here.

The sun was coming at a low angle through the brigalow and lighting the side of his face. I noticed for the first time his eyes was a kind of blue colour, but a bit on the watery side. I did not think his threat was convincing. I seen the weakness of it in his watery blue eyes and I despised him. He might be forced to it by his own weakness and his wife's craziness. That thought did worry me a little. My injured wrist was throbbing and my mouth was filled with saliva from the whack he give me. I turned my head aside and spat into the sand and I swallowed some saliva and spat again. This man would never have hit me that way if I had not been manacled. He pushed the point of the Webley's barrel against the side of my nose and turned my head towards him. I looked at him and I said, You hit me one more time, Mr Collins, and I will have nothing more to say to you or to Mrs Collins. You are a weak man and a bully. I have no confidence in you. I do not know what you mean by my plan. I do not have no plan. If Ben Tobin was going to get his revenge on you he would have done it in his own time without needing me to back him up. I looked aside and spat again. My spit was red where my cheek had cut on the inside against my teeth. I said, Ben Tobin never needed no one to back him up, not me nor anyone.

Daniel stood up. We shall see, he said. I seen he was forming up a plan of his own now. That is the way such people think. There is nothing straight in their own minds, so they think there is nothing straight in the minds of other people. He looked at Esme where she was sitting on the scuffed-up sand with her head in her hands. I said to myself, There is a lost man and he will come undone. Nothing is surer. He said to his wife, who was looking like some poor old relative of Rosie's after a night on the wine, We must get back to the station, Ez. Do you think you are up to it? He went over and crouched beside her and put his arm around her shoulders and spoke to her. She was not crying. I could see that much. I could not say what she was thinking and I do not care to speculate on it. My face was aching where he hit me. I did not care much about their feelings just then.

I looked over at them, studying the way they was, and I knew there was nothing more certain than them two was not going to find their way back to the Mount Hay police house through the scrubs without me to guide them there. They would be going around in circles till they was too done up to go no further, then they would sit down just like them old piker bullocks when they was winded from being chased, and they would never get up again but would lay there and give in to their despair. That is how it is. I sat on the ground looking at them thinking a lot of thoughts that come into my head just then. One thought I had was, So what if I refuse to get up? What if I let them go off and lose themselves in the scrubs and they are never heard of again? As I thought of them two perishing in the scrubs I seen a picture of the wild pigs and the dogs dragging their bones about and scattering them like they do with the carcasses of cattle and old roos. I would not need to do nothing criminal to them but just tell them, I am not walking back with my hands manacled and my face beat up. It is not me who drove your daughter away but you yourselves who done it to her. I would tell him, I owe you nothing. You cuffed me and you beat me, all for nothing but your own panic and suspicion, and now you are on your own, Daniel Collins. Let us see how you go without Bobby Blue looking after you out here. I reckoned I could be at Ben's place by morning and he would get the cuffs off me. Then me and Irie could head out to the spring of the old fig tree. Ben would lend us a couple of horses and stores. I tried thinking how I might get Mother and my saddle but I could not see no way of doing it that made sense. Ben would go in and get Mother for me one night and bring her out to the fig tree. The four of us would have a fine time camped there together for a few days until me and Irie worked something out for our future. I could see no further than that. But I knew I had committed no crime and had nothing to be ashamed of. All I had to fear was being misunderstood by these people from the coast. The authorities was on their side and would come hunting for me and Irie, for sure, but that would be better than this and when they caught up with us one day we would have nothing to confess to them but our own happiness at being with each other. We was both at home in the scrubs. She was right about that and was a natural for this country. I had been a fool not to take her to the spring of the fig tree when she come up with her plan and we had a chance to make a clean getaway then. I should have trusted to her judgment. I felt good thinking about Irie. I would make it up with her and prove I was reliable for her. I regretted my failure to respect her plan. Regret for my foolishness is what it was. I like to be honest with myself and not lie about such things. My mother will never have nothing to be ashamed of from me. I know that.

Daniel lifted Esme onto her feet and they come over to me and he got behind me and put his hands under my arms and hauled me up. Get going! I leaned back at him. I am not going nowhere, I said. If you want to go back to the police house you had better be making a start or it will be dark before you get there. I am staying here, I said. I looked him steady in the eye. I have had enough of walking around in the scrubs without no hands being beaten on by you because you do not trust your daughter. I am done with it.

I seen a look of doubt come into those pale blue eyes of his and I thought, I have got him. Get these cuffs off me, I said, and I will think about maybe taking you back. But I am not doing it cuffed. Esme stepped up and said, Don't free him, Dan. He'll make a bolt for it and leave us here. Daniel looked at me. You can stay here if you want to, he said. I will strip you naked and tie you to that tree right behind you so you stay here till we come back and pick you up. He smiled. That is if we can find you again in this godforsaken place. I said, I do not see nothing for you to tie me with. He said straight up, like he had already thought it out and was pleased with himself, Your clothes will rip up and do nicely. I said, You will get lost on your own. He said, Maybe we will. And that will be just too bad for you tied up here waiting for us. You might remember, he said, getting cocky with it now, I found my way back to the police house in Mount Hay from that trash hole of your mate's place out at Coal Creek. And that was at night. A dark night too. Now you have brought us here and you are the one wearing those handcuffs, not me. If I know anything, you will be showing us the way back. So you see, I am not such a sorry creature as you imagine me to be. It is you doing my bidding, not the other way around.

I said, That old horse Finisher found your way home for you. You was as bushed as a baby rabbit. I seen your tracks wavering all over the place out there by the red wall. But you are not on a horse today, Mr Collins. And you will die in these scrubs just the same as I will if you leave me here tied to this tree. He said, Well let us see which of us is right, shall we, you or me? He stepped up to me and loosed the buckle of my belt and smiled into my face like he knew he had won. I said, All right. I will take you back. He stepped away. Let's go then. I said, Do up my belt. He did it up. I said, I have committed no crime. You have no right to hold me in these cuffs. Daniel stepped back and said, How about conspiracy to kidnap my children? Is that crime enough for you? He was sneering at me when he said this and I did not like to hear it and I got a scare from it. I said, Your daughter will tell you there is no such thing as a conspiracy. To leave you was her idea and she done it on her own. He said nothing to this but pushed me forward roughly and told me to get going.

As I went along, making my way up the stony incline, I thought about what he had said. It had come as a shock to me and I began to see the way them two was intending to take this whole thing. They had the authorities with them and could make anything they liked to make of it. I tried to believe it would all be cleared up and understood when we caught up with Irie at Ben's place, but I could no longer trust to that view of how it was to go. I could not wait to get there now and to hear her backing me up and telling these two the truth of this whole thing.

. . .

Later on I turned around when I could no longer hear them and I seen Daniel and Esme was fallen a long way behind me. He called to me to hold up and wait for them. When they come on I seen Esme was having some kind of asthma attack and finding it hard to get her breath. I waited and watched them. From being friendly at the beginning, them two now seemed to me to be the most dangerous people I had ever got myself tangled up with. When it began to get dark I thought of giving them the slip and doubling back and making my way out to Coal Creek. But the truth is I lacked the spirit for that. I could have lost them two easily in the dark, or even in the daylight, handcuffed or not, but I knew I would have spent the rest of my life haunted by their helpless struggle to survive out there. They was the kind of people needed a torch to see where they was going and I was their torch. I knew I could not abandon them. But I wished I could.

I stood and waited for them again. In some stupid way they seemed to me like children. I had never seen two people more in the wrong place than them two. I hoped they would be going back down the coast once they got their girls back. But I did not like to think too closely on this, as I was afraid me and Irie would be split up whichever way this thing went and would never see each other again. I was not so stupid I did not see she was the best thing ever come into my life or ever likely to come into it.

My right wrist had swelled up onto the cuffs and was giving me some gee-up. I thought maybe the skin had split. I had a deep ache for a cigarette and for something in my belly. I had gone without food for a day before this but I had never gone without a smoke. As I went along through the dimlit scrub, that long day dying around us, I dreamed of finding myself alone with Daniel Collins and the two of us fighting it out. And in my dream I beat him till he lay on the ground bloodied and pleading to me to forgive him all the wrongs he done to me. This little dream of getting my vengeance of him kept my spirits up.

But it is given only to the prophets to see the future before its time and is not given to us to know what is to become of us. And that may be just as well, for we can dream in the present and see no harm in it but get our comfort from our dreams, and if we could see the future we would have no dreams but only the wreck of our days to think on.

ELEVEN

The quarter moon had been down already more than an hour by the time I come up to the horse paddock and the night sky was just giving way to the first sign of the dawn, a chill greyness over the world, a low mist rising on the open ground. We had been doing a lot of stopping to rest for Esme in the night and there was times I thought she was not going to make it no further. They was off behind me some way and I squirmed under the bottom wire without their help. Tip had been barking steadily ever since she first heard us approaching through the scrub. But she did not come to meet us. Bark-bark-bark, she went, kind of flat and with nothing of a welcome in it. There was something sad in the sound of Tip's bark and I did not like to hear it. I wondered that she did not come down to greet us. When I come through the horse paddock the horses was keeping still and quiet. I could see them bunched up in the bottom corner of the paddock staring in my direction with their big startled eyes. Esme must have got hung up on the wire coming through some way behind me; I heard her cry out, a wretched kind of cry in the dismal morning, like a mare struggling in trouble to give birth, no human word in it but something animal and exhausted. I waited by the shed till they come up to me.

He was coaxing her along and near to carrying her. She was having trouble with her breathing and seemed to be close to collapsing. She rested against the door getting her breath and he told me to get into the back of the jeep. When I was in he manacled me to the handhold above the wheel housing. When he had me fastened he reached in and took out the .303. I watched them two struggling across to the house, her hanging off his arm wheezing like some old pump, the .303 slung over his shoulder the way a soldier would carry his gun. And I remembered he had been in the army in New Guinea before he joined the police and come up to the ranges. Seeing him like that in his stained shirt and pants with that gun he looked like a soldier would look who had been out in some battle all night and was coming back with a wounded comrade. The lights went on over at the house and I heard their voices. Tip had stopped barking and was giving out a kind of whining sound that went off into a bit of a howl every now and then.

I snapped awake when I slid off the guard and the cuffs jerked tight. Both my wrists was swollen and bleeding and I cried out with the sudden pain of it. I seen the light was on in the office, Daniel's shadow against the window. He was talking on the telephone, his voice was raised but I could not hear what he was saying. I had a headache and was feeling pretty low. I did not see how we could ever be normal with each other again. No matter what Irie was to tell them I knew we had gone too far into something else to ever turn it around. These two was the kind of people who was never going to apologise to a hired man like me. They was no longer treating me with the decency any man or woman should get. There was no way back on it.

They come out and crossed over towards me. She was carrying George Wilson's old twelve-gauge shotgun, a bunch of spare shells clinking in the front pocket of her apron as she climbed into the passenger seat at the front. From being a young and friendly woman, Esme Collins had taken on the look of an old deranged woman with nothing in her mind but a picture of her daughters in captivity to the violent and cruel man she believed Ben Tobin to be, a mixture of terror and crazy determination in her to get them girls of hers back. She was gripping on to that old gun of George's like she thought it was the hand of her Saviour. I could have told her the right barrel of that weapon was inclined to misfire, as the spring was weakened, but she was not a woman to be spoken to with reason. Daniel was wearing his slouch hat with the strap under his chin. I noticed the flap on the holster of his Webley was fastened down. It looked like he had got himself smartened up to be the real boss of this and the authority in charge of how it was to go. I knew that even with his girls still lost to him he would be thinking of writing his report to his superiors on the coast. Making a big man of himself out here in what he seen as the wild country but anyone in Mount Hay could have told him was the quiet country. I would say they had both had a drink of something as I could smell liquor on them. He kept the .303 in the front with him between the seats. I reckoned that phone call of his would have been to the coast. Who else would he be calling on the telephone at this hour but his headquarters people? They said nothing to me but sat up front, her with that old open-hammer shotgun of George's across her legs.

It was nearing sunup by the time we headed out but he put on his lights anyway and they danced and flickered on the scrub ahead of us. My backside was getting battered from the bumping around. I was near to passing out a couple of times with the pain in my wrists, which was gone all up my arms and across my chest. Daniel slowed up whenever he come on dual tracks, and he yelled out to me, Which track? I told him and he took off with a violent jerk and flew along for some way till the tracks confused him again. And so it went on until I yelled to him to slow down. The sun was up now, knifing at eye level through the timber, and we was just about on the lip of the Coal Creek crossing. The creek was still running but with no more than a foot or two of water in it. Daniel put the jeep in low low and we got over and climbed out on the silt with no trouble. Despite the cool air of the morning I was sweating with pain and with my worry. Daniel drove up to about twenty yards off the front door of Ben's place and cut the motor.

. . .

I have told about what happened next in detail many times at the trial and since that day. I have always been careful to tell it as it was. What I seen was not the way Esme spoke of it afterwards. Esme's was a different story to mine. At the trial there was a number of different versions given of what happened that morning outside Ben Tobin's place on Coal Creek, but I stuck to what I seen and I have never changed nothing of my story. The name Coal Creek was never the same afterwards. I know what I seen. This was it.

The jeep was a left-hand drive and Esme was sitting right there in front of me on the seat next to Daniel. She jumped out of the jeep before it come to a stop and tripped and went to her knees. She went down hard and that old gun of George Wilson's flew out of her hands and landed out ahead of her in the dirt. When she looked up the first thing she seen was Ben at the door of his place. She claimed to have thought he was coming for her and she was in fear of her life. She scrambled forward on her knees and grabbed for that old gun and she swung it up and let go with the left barrel without taking aim, just firing in a blind panic. The main bunch of shot sent splinters flying off the side of the door, the spread catching Ben in his side so that he spun around and snatched at the lintel to hold himself steady. He was very evidently not expecting to get shot. I seen the look of surprise on his face. He steadied himself a moment before he reached in and grabbed that single-shot .22 pea rifle of his that he kept behind the door for the snakes. He then stepped out just one step from the door with the rifle held sideways in his hands, not pointing it at no one but yelling something which I do not remember, just a wild kind of yell, like he was trying to hold the situation up till he could work out what was going on.

Two things happened at once then. When the shotgun blasted, Irie come out of the house down behind the galley with Deeds hanging on to her. Irie was screaming, Mummm! over and over. Her mother was still on her knees with the twelve-gauge in her hands and maybe Irie thought her mother had been shot. Daniel was already out of the jeep. I seen him fumbling with the buckle on the holster of that Webley and I remembered the picture I had of George Wilson when I was a boy, that old man struggling to get out his gun while the bad man shot him to his knees. But that is not what happened. Daniel got the gun in his hand and began to shoot at Ben. Bang-bang-bang, three shots in a row, I still hear them, not steadying himself or aiming the gun but just holding it out in front of him and firing it off, his face screwed up and yelling something back at Ben. Maybe cursing. I cannot say for sure. When Irie screamed, Esme turned towards her and screamed back at her to get inside. Daniel was firing his Webley revolver at Ben and Ben lifted the pea rifle and let go his one shot. I could see Daniel was panicked and did not coolly take aim and he missed Ben altogether, which was not hard for him to do. As Daniel pulled off his third shot Miriam jumped out from behind Ben in the doorway and Daniel's third shot took her in the chest and knocked her over backwards. At almost the same instant Ben's single shot hit Daniel in the side of his skull and Daniel went down.

So long as I live I will never forget the sight of young Miriam going over backwards and kind of bouncing when she hit the hard pack of that anthill floor in Ben's place. It still makes me sick in the guts to remember the way that kid went down. Like she was made of rubber. When I turned back to Daniel I seen Ben's one shot had caught him in the side of his head. He was on his face, blood coming out of his head. I looked back at Ben and he had dropped the pea rifle and was kneeling at Miriam. I do not know if it was being shot in the side with them pellets that was making him kneel or if he was trying to revive the child. Esme let go her second barrel at him but it misfired as it generally would do. George never used the right barrel.

That is what I remember clearly. Others did not remember it the way I did. But I know what I saw. I remember other things too, but not so clearly as them first few seconds of it. But I do remember Esme being in the doorway of Ben's place holding Miriam's head in her hands and kind of rocking up and down and screaming to her child, and Irie being up there with her and crying out and pawing at her mother. And I remember thinking what a child she was. When I looked around I seen Daniel was moving and had shifted his head on one side. His eyes was open and I was glad he was not dead. His lips was moving and I guess he was saying something, or trying to. That slouch hat of his was knocked clean off and was lying out in the yard on its own, drifting backwards and forwards on its stiff brim in the morning breeze. I remember that. Ben always said when he seen Mrs Collins go down the first time he was intending to head across and help her to her feet. He said her shooting him was not expected. But she claimed he menaced her with his rifle and that is why she shot him, in fear of her life, she said she was. Which was a term the police used. And it may be true, for she was a woman in a state of fear and panic and extreme exhaustion already when we pulled up at Ben's place and was not in no mood for acting reasonably and sitting around talking about nothing. Especially her kids. But the way I remember it she fired off that old shotgun of George's before Ben reached for the .22 behind the door.

I do not say Esme was lying about her reason for shooting at Ben and maybe she thought she was telling the truth. But I do know if she had not fired that old gun of George's the rest of it would not have happened the way it did. It might have happened some other way. But not that way. That much is for sure. Everyone who heard the story at the trial seen a picture of a mother that morning on her knees before the cruel menace of the animal who had kidnapped her children. She claimed she pulled that trigger in desperation and self-defence. I do not know how many times she said that. There was a lot of other things that was said later on about what happened that morning out at Coal Creek that was not true, but by then that day and the name Coal Creek had become a kind of dark legend among the people on the coast in which the widow and her dead husband was the heroes and the real truth was long buried with little Miriam and her dad.

. . .

I was manacled to that jeep and I was not able to move and I seen it all, or mostly all of it. I could not be looking two ways at once and do not recall seeing Daniel get out of the jeep. But he was out and not far behind Esme and his first shot come close behind hers. It was all over in a few seconds and takes a lot longer to tell than it did to happen. All our lives was changed forever in them few confused seconds of panic and none of it should have ever happened. Ben was all set to bring them two kids back to their mother and father that morning. I believe that to be true. If Ben had had the chance to do it his way, it would have been an opportunity for him and the Collins to reach some kind of trust and even a friendship. Them people might have learned something about themselves and the people of the ranges. Laying in my bunk at Stuart, the racket that was always going on in that place keeping me from sleep in them early days, I often imagined a scene of Ben driving up to the police house in his old International truck, Tip jumping at the wheels and them two girls sitting up alongside him having the adventure of their lives and waving out the side window. In these night imaginings Esme come out of the police house wearing her apron and was overjoyed to see her girls safe with Ben. She invited him into the kitchen to have breakfast with the family. I smiled to myself to see them all laughing and telling their stories together, like it was some great adventure they all shared. The way I daydreamed it many times, the story of our lives had a happy ending. But that was not the way it was in real life and there are yet some things I must tell about here before this whole story of it is done with.

TWELVE

Me and Ben was separated away from each other in Stuart. When the story come out in the newspapers we was shown as evil villains without no conscience or concern for our fellow creatures. The papers give it out that Ben Tobin and his well-known associate, Robert Blewitt, alias Bobby Blue, had been terrorising the law-abiding residents of Mount Hay township for years, where they was known for their cruelty. On arriving in the town the newly appointed constable, Daniel Collins, a decorated veteran of the Australian campaign in New Guinea, where he served with distinction as corporal, decided to bring to account the likes of Tobin and his associates. Constable Collins went out on his own to Tobin's hideout at Coal Creek in the wild scrubs and arrested him and brought him to justice for abusing a young Aboriginal girl. When Tobin swore to get his vengeance on Constable Collins after he come out of prison, so the story in the newspapers said, him and his accomplice, Robert Blewitt, made the plan of getting the trust of the Collins family so they could arrange the kidnap and molesting of the two innocent young Collins girls as payback on Constable Collins.

No mention was made that it was the same Constable Collins who accidentally shot dead his own child out at Coal Creek on account of Mrs Collins firing off a shotgun at Ben Tobin without no reason in the first place. At the centre of the story the papers told about Coal Creek was the grieving mother of the dead little girl and the widow of Constable Daniel Collins, the war hero. Esme's suffering and grief and her courage was the big story for them. Much was made of her heroism in wounding the villain Ben Tobin before he shot her husband dead. There was a photograph of Mrs Esme Collins dressed in black with a veil over her face holding the hand of her surviving child, Irie, at the funeral in Townsville of her murdered husband and their youngest child, Miriam. This photograph of a mother's grief caused a great stir and there was howls from ordinary people looking to avenge her. Esme was shown to be a woman of great courage and a deep and generous care for the welfare of the community of Mount Hay.

A couple of days after we was admitted into remand a crowd was gathered outside the gates of the gaol. They was chanting and waving placards and calling for the death sentence for Ben and me. I think if the police had let us go free, that crowd would have hanged us anyway. We was said to be the most heartless criminals ever known in the district. Once the people had that story from the newspapers there was no going back to the truth of it for me and Ben. One newspaper even called it the Coal Creek Massacre. Which was plain stupid and wrong. The newspapers lied and twisted the truth around to make people get excited. Which is what people did. They was all townspeople with a natural fear of the bush and was always looking for some sensational event to come out of the wild country up there in the ranges. It did not make no difference to them that for the whole time George Wilson was the constable at Mount Hay they had never heard of no trouble out there. Most people had never heard of Mount Hay before this, including the newspapers, so what could they know of it? Something like the idea of the Coal Creek Massacre did not surprise them but only made them more sure they had been right all along to believe that country was lawless and filled with brutal types of men. If I had been asked I would have said it was partly the Collinses' own original expectation of adventure and sensational events in the ranges that caused the whole thing to get out of hand and go the way it did. They had no need to go putting me in handcuffs and beating on me that day. I would have taken them out there and found their girls without no trouble if they had not panicked but had given me a chance. And I never heard of no one taking a shotgun to a neighbour in Mount Hay before Esme did it.

I had been in Stuart no more than a few days when I got a message through one of the guards from George Wilson letting me know Chiller was taking care of Mother and the other horses at the police house, and he had Tip over there at the pub with him. He said nothing of Deeds and I do not know if Ben had any news of her. Once we was in the gaol me and Ben did not see each other until the trial got going, and then only to nod.

. . .

The side of the story that never did get into the newspapers was how Ben took charge after the shooting and got us all back to the police house in Mount Hay that morning. When we arrived back at the police house in the jeep from Coal Creek, the Flying Doctor plane and their people was waiting there to meet us. There was two detectives come out from the coast with the Flying Doctor and they was waiting to arrest me and Ben, which they did without asking us no questions. Daniel had called the police headquarters when we come back in the night from seeing the girls' and Ben's and Deeds' tracks at the rock shelter. That was the phone call I seen him making. He asked for help and for the Flying Doctor service to come out, as he and Esme was in great fear their girls would have been injured in some way, and there was no doctor in Mount Hay. I do not know what they thought Ben was going to do to them girls and they never did say, but only give the impression it was something evil.

Esme and Daniel and the body of Miriam, along with Irie, was all flown down to the hospital in Townsville and me and Ben was left cuffed in the cell at the police office in Mount Hay in the care of them two detectives. The part of the story that never got told was that it was Ben drove the jeep in from Coal Creek and him who helped Esme get Daniel into the back of it. Ben was calm and Esme was in no state to see any sense or do nothing for herself. Ben's side was giving him pain where the pellets had tore into him but he did not mind his own pain and took the responsibility of getting that family back to help as soon as he could. Ben was a cool head to have onside when you was in trouble. I knew that from experience with him. Daniel died the following morning in the Townsville hospital. When this news come through on the telephone to the detectives they come down to the cell and charged Ben and me with murder. We was already charged with conspiracy to kidnap minors and some other charges they made up and which I now forget. They said I was Ben's accomplice and was just as guilty as he was of murdering Constable Collins. I did not like the feeling it give me to be charged with murder but I did not make no protest against it. I was with Ben no matter which way it went. I knew that.

When the detectives had finished with us and had left us, Ben said, If you kill a policeman there is no hope for you but hanging. I still thought the truth would come out and we would be let go and maybe even thanked for being so helpful. I said, Irie will tell them all what happened and clear it up for us. Ben laughed at me for this idea. And I soon learned what an innocent fool I was to ever think like that. The facts was just as twisted around and exaggerated at the trial as they was in the newspapers. At first me and Ben laughed at the way the prosecution told the story, then we got used to hearing it and stopped listening. The lawyer the state give us was a man by the name of Alfred Katzen, which I thought was an unusual name, which is why I remember it. Alfred told us plainly we was in for it and to get our minds set for the worst outcome. He smelled of grog and was tired of life himself. He was a man my father would have scorned to speak to. I felt sorry for him and did not think he was such a bad sort, just someone whose luck had deserted him early in life. He told me he had received threats to his life if he got us off. He smiled when he said this. I don't think there's much hope of that happening, Bobby, he said. I told him not to worry about it as I had already seen how things was to go with us.

. . .

In the cell at the police office in Mount Hay the detectives had us both in cuffs and they give us a beating, which they said was for resisting arrest. Which was a lie. We knew they beat us because one of their own people had been killed and they needed to take out their revenge on us. Until we went into the gaol them two had us in their power and could do with us just as they wished to do. On the drive in to the coast they talked between themselves about shooting us and I believe they would have done it if they had thought they could get away with it. Ben knew how to laugh at them, which made them fierce with him. But I just took it and ground my teeth. Ben had learned in childhood that taking a beating is nothing so very special anyway and they could make no impression on him, which got them wild.

During the twelve-hour ride to the coast they took turns at the wheel of the jeep. I was in severe pain with my wrists and Ben was sliding into being unconscious from the beating they give him and from his shotgun wound. We was still in cuffs. They took Ben's tobacco from him and did not give us nothing to eat. I had no tobacco on me to get taken, but I would not have been able to roll a smoke anyway with my hands behind my back. If I'd had some tobacco I would have tried. While we was driving to the coast I worried what was to happen to Mother and Tip while I was away, and I know Ben was worried what was to happen to Deeds left out there at Coal Creek on her own and pregnant with their child.

I had had nothing to eat for a couple of days at that time and very little to drink and I was not in a good way for thinking clearly about nothing except wanting a smoke. When we got to Townsville I did not get no treatment in the remand cell for the wounds on my wrists from wearing those cuffs. My right wrist become infected and I could not sleep for the throbbing pain of it. The poison went up my arm and ulcerated. I still carry the scar of it.

. . .

They said our trial was a bigger event in Townsville than the annual show and rodeo. I was described as a weak man and a willing follower of Ben Tobin's evil schemes. I was led by him, so they said, into the heinous crimes that he planned to get his revenge back on Constable Collins for being sent to prison. Ben told the plain truth of it and if they had listened to him they would have seen the whole thing was a mistake and a result of the Collinses' panic about their daughters and the Collinses' ignorance of the ways of settling things in the ranges. Ben said straight up, We was riding back through the scrubs from visiting Deeds' relatives in Mount Hay when we come on the girls in the rock shelter. The smaller of the two girls, Miriam, the one her dad shot dead, was crying and wailing and the other one, the older one, was calm and steady but worried all the same by being lost. Me and Deeds took the girls up behind us on our horses and rode home to our place on Coal Creek with them and Deeds put them to bed and calmed the younger one. We did not have the telephone at our place, Ben told them, and it was our intention to take the girls back to the police house in the morning after we had given them their breakfast. They was both still sleeping when the constable and his wife come up in the jeep and the wife started blasting at me with that old shotgun of George Wilson's. Ben said he was sincerely sorry the .22 bullet had killed Daniel Collins but that he was being fired at by Collins at the time and did not expect a single shot from that pea rifle to kill him but only to make him duck away and give himself a half second to dive out of the firing line. It was an unlucky shot, he said, or a lucky one, depending on how you looked at it, as the constable was going to keep on firing and must have hit me sooner or later with one of them big .38 bullets. But no one in the court was paying attention to what

Ben was saying and they all just thought he was making up some yarn to save his own skin. The way they would have lied themselves in his position. But Ben was not lying. He was just saying it the way it was. He knew there was no hope of saving his own skin.

Irie did not show up to set them straight. The Collins family was described as good Christian people, the husband a war hero and gentle father, and the mother a worker for the good of the Mount Hay community, where she revived the tennis club and the women's social association and helped to defend the Aboriginal women against the brutality of men like Ben Tobin. The Collinses was an unselfish and civilised family, an ideal kind of family they seemed when their lawyer described them, people with only the good of the community and the welfare of their girls in their hearts. Which I dare say was true. Just like the good people of Townsville themselves. It was the kindness and the trusting natures of the Collins family that Robert Blewitt (that was me) took advantage of, and which he then betrayed with the most heartless indecency, luring their daughters into the bush and leading them to where Ben Tobin could capture them and take them to his hideout in the wild scrubs for his own indecent purposes. They never said what those indecent purposes was but everyone thought they knew what they was, because that was what was in their own minds. It sickened me to my guts to hear them say it. I seen my brother

Charley sitting in the court one day and when I looked at him he looked down into his lap and I seen he was ashamed to be my kin. I was glad in the end I did not see Irie in the court and she did not have to sit there listening to all that indecent talk. If I had seen her in the court I know I would have felt different about things. Her not being there made it easier for me in a way I did not expect.

. . .

After hearing it said in the court again and again I began in the end to half believe what they was saying about me and Ben and to think that maybe it was the truth after all. I found it hard to remember exactly what the real truth was and to untangle it in my mind from the lies and exaggerations. I got confused giving my replies to the lawyer. I even found I was wanting to agree with him after a while just to get it over and done with and to make things easier for everyone. I just wanted to say yes to everything he asked me and be done with the madness of it all. The jury was out less than an hour and when they come back and said they had found me and Ben guilty of all the charges against us the people in the court stood up and clapped and cheered. I felt a kind of relief in myself at the verdict. It is hard to imagine it now, but at the time I remember feeling I was only getting my due after all. It was like I just wanted to be as convinced of my guilt as everyone else was. Two weeks later me and Ben was brought back to the court to be sentenced.

The court was crowded with people wanting to hear the worst for us. There was a waiting silence when the clerk of the court come up behind the judge and held a square of black cloth over the top of the judge's wig, spread out between his two hands, and the judge looked at me and Ben in the dock with our guards and told us we was to hang. I looked at Ben and he smiled and I was glad I was going with him and was not to stay behind on my own. By that time I had lost my dreams of ever again having a decent life and I had no care in me for my own life. Going with Ben was the best thing in my idea of how it was to be for me just then. They did not set a date for the hanging, but I did not care one way or the other. It was out of my hands and it would soon be over. That was all. Somehow it seemed right the way it was. I had no fear of my own death. If someone had told me a few months earlier I was going to die in three weeks or ten days I would have run a mile. Now it did not affect me except to make me feel quiet inside, like the trial had emptied the lake of my life and I was just the mud on the bottom drying in the sun. It all meant nothing to me at that time, which I suppose was a state of shock.

. . .

Later on I changed this view, but I had come to it at that time and I felt no fear or despair when the judge said them words. I thought to myself, Well this is it then, Bobby. You are done with this life and like the judge said you must trust in the mercy of the Lord for the next. If I had been given the chance that day I would have thanked the judge for his words. I had no ill feelings for him, and I believe he had none for us. We was all just playing our parts in it and it did not matter somehow that it was not true. The truth got lost and we forgot what it was. The account of what took place out at Coal Creek had got so twisted up and rearranged during the trial I was pretty well convinced I deserved what I was to get for my part in it. But I was not convinced I was evil. I was never convinced of that. I seen that good and evil did not count in the law but only if you was found guilty or not guilty. And me and Ben was found guilty. It all come down to that.

Miriam and her dad was dead, there was no arguing with that, and we had all played some part in bringing about their deaths. Esme and Irie was to suffer their loss for the rest of their lives and it did not seem unfair that me and Ben was to also suffer an equal loss. I did not look at Esme when the judge said his words. And I was glad Irie was not in the court to hear them said that day. I knew I did not belong to their world no more and I did not crave the impossible, to be rejoined to it, nor did I regret nothing.

My death was all of one piece inside me at that moment, a cool empty place like them playgrounds of the Old Murri people, shining as a silk dress in the starlight. I probably smiled to think of that. The regret I had which did not slip away was to lose Mother. It pained me to think of her.

THIRTEEN

My brother Charley come to the prison to visit me the week after we was sentenced. He brought me my mother's Bible and her red silk scarf that I had kept it wrapped in. I sniffed the scarf but it had lost the smell of her hair and I knew she was absent from me in that place. Knowing my mother's absence from me I let the place get me down for a while. Charley had got the Bible and the scarf along with my saddle and my other gear from the police as my only kin. The detectives had searched my few possessions at the Mount Hay quarters and confiscated them. Charley handed the Bible across to me and said, You were always her favourite, and he smiled to show there was no hard feelings between us in him saying this. It was true. He was my brother and though he was something of a stranger to me I could do nothing but love him.

He was wearing a smart grey suit and tie and he had a new brown hat that he held by the brim between his fingers, just like he had in the court. He had grown a moustache, which was not as red as his hair but had brown in it and small touches of grey. He looked prosperous and a man of the town. You could see nothing of the ranges in him. We did not speak of him leaving the family at a young age but I seen it had not been to his disadvantage and he had become the man he wanted to become. He did not ask, but I thought to give him an account of our mother's funeral and how all the town followed the coffin up the hill behind the dam. He did not move while I told him this but sat looking down at that hat in his hands. So I spared him an account of Dad's passing. But I told him to sell my saddle and our dad's gear and to ask Chiller to keep Mother and not to sell her. I did not want no one riding that mare. He said he would do these things but I never found out if he did them and I never seen no money from him selling my gear and my dad's stuff, which I was sorry to think of leaving my care as I had always thought I would cherish it till my own end. But some things are not to be as we expect them to be. I do not hold no feeling against Charley. He had become a stranger to our ways and made his own life and I respected that in him.

We was like strangers sitting there in the prison and we soon ran out of things to say to each other and sat in silence, him turning the hat by the brim and looking down, and me looking at him. I said, I believe you have a wife and children? He come back to life at the mention of his family and told me he had two girls and a boy and they was all in school and doing well. His job was managing the office at the McKay sugar mill. They had bought themselves a house out at Farleigh, he said. But I did not know where that was and had no picture of it in my mind. Before he left he give me his cigarettes and said he would come again and was there anything else I particularly wanted? I seen he was eager to go and was uncomfortable in the prison with me, so I said there was nothing I wanted and I thanked him for coming to see me. I never seen him again.

. . .

After the sentencing me and Ben was put in two of the three condemned cells at Stuart. They was up on the second floor at the back of the main gallery, the one empty cell between us. We was not allowed to call out to each other and the doors was too thick to hear if we was just speaking. Ben played his Hohner most evenings and I could hear that okay. I lay on my bunk with my eyes closed and listened to his version of The Wild Colonial Boy, which he knew was just about my favourite song, especially the lines, *He was his father's only hope, his mother's pride and joy.* We was neither of us wild colonial boys but we liked that song. I could not hear them lines without thinking of my mother. Ben sang a line then broke off and give a few melancholy bars on the mouth organ then come in again with the words, adding in little flourishes on the Hohner here and there. I lay on my bunk with my eyes closed listening to him playing and imagining a time with me and Irie and him and Deeds camped out at the spring of the old fig tree together, a big fire shooting sparks into a sky full of stars and us all having a good time.

After the judge set a date for Ben's hanging the days went by quickly. They come to take him down to the execution place at five in the morning. It was still dark and I was awake and heard them open his cell. Ho there, Bobby, he called out to me. And he laughed that good old scary laugh of his that I knew would send a shiver through them guards. They are going to hang me, Bobby. I could not laugh but I called back, I love you, Ben. I love you too, Bobby Blue, he called and then the door slammed behind them and they was gone. They was our last words to each other. Good words they was. Ben Tobin was not a saint, but he was not an evil man neither. They should have let him see Deeds before he died but they said she was not his kin and had no rights.

After Ben went down the stairs and we heard the door bang closed on him one of the prisoners in the gallery started singing The Wild Colonial Boy. Gradually all the men joined in, until they was all singing like a loud challenging chant of the song, as if it was the war cry of a crazy horde of warriors. *There was a wild colonial boy, Ben Tobin was his name*, they sung. And I seen how they was making a legend and a hero for themselves out of Ben. The singing went on for some time then it suddenly stopped like someone had cut it off. The stones of the prison trembled with that silence.

I was standing by the door of my cell waiting, my blood whooshing in my ears. I nearly jumped out of my skin when the shutter on my door banged open. The guard placed Ben's dinted old Hohner on the plate and when I reached for it he said, Your mate hangs on the bell, Bobby Blue. And that was what the silence of the men was for. They knew it and was waiting for the bell. I stood by the door holding Ben's mouth organ and I prayed to the Lord Jesus Christ our Saviour to take him to him and keep him until the time I was to go over and join him and all those others waiting over there. When the bell struck I hung my head and wept for my friend and I said in my mind, They hung the Lord Jesus on the cross too, Ben, and my mother's voice come to me then, soft and gentle as the palm of her hand to my cheek,

We all hang on the cross, Bobby Blue. We all hang on the cross. And I thought how lonely Ben must have been down there in that place where they hanged men, them judges and newspaper men and Gillen Dawes, the governor, all standing around to see him go. I know he would have smiled at them and they would never have seen his sorrow for the loss of Deeds and their child. Ben would never have let them see his sorrow. I know that. They was hanging a little child's father and no one was to come to any good from them doing it. I loved Ben and will love him until the day I go over to the other side and join them all assembled there. This true account of what happened is for his memory after all them people who hated him and saw him as an evil man are dead and gone themselves. I have another reason too for writing this, which I will speak of.

. . .

My friend Ben was dead and I was never to see him ever again. When I closed my eyes I could see his smile and hear his voice. Now I thought I was for the rope within a week or two of his hanging, and I did not mind one bit but was impatient to go and be done with it all. I had seen the eye of death in that pea rifle Ben shot Daniel Collins with when Deeds had it pointed at my eye, and I had known the beckoning of that place beyond the dawn. I did not mind the thought of it and had no fear. I read the Gospels each night and thought of my mother reading them same words to me and Dad. Then Alfred come and seen me and told me he was appealing my death sentence now that the heat had gone out of the iron of vengeance and people was feeling satisfied that the ringleader of the horrors, as they called them, of Coal Creek had paid the ultimate price.

That is what he called being hanged: the ultimate price. Alfred had letters from George Wilson and Chiller Swales giving me a good character but he had not been able to use them at the trial as it was said they was not material to the case. He was going to use these character references to help in appealing my death sentence. I told Alfred, I do not want no appeal. I am ready to go. He would not listen to me but said I was young and would change my mind on death given a chance, and he went ahead anyway and my sentence was commuted to life. Which he said meant twenty years if I behaved myself. In spite of the great differences between us I think me and Alfred liked each other. He give me a hug when he come to tell me I would not hang and I smelled the stink of the stale grog on his breath. He said, You are a young man, Bobby. When you come out of this place I will be long gone ahead of you. I told him it was no good predicting the future, as we could not see our way to it.

. . .

I was sorry at that time they did not send me down with Ben, but once I had my life back in my hands I seen Alfred was right and I soon forgot I had ever wished for my own end and began to value my life again and to have hopes for myself. I learned a lot about myself in that time and have not forgotten them lessons. When my sentence was commuted I was taken before Governor Dawes for an interview. He stayed sitting down at his desk looking at me over his glasses for some moments, then he said, Take them cuffs off the boy. He's not going to run away on us. And he laughed and smoked his cigarette. The guard removed my handcuffs. Dawes was not a bad man, I believe, he just had a lot of bad men to deal with and was let down many times in the trust he give them. He still believed in his own quiet judgment of the people he was in charge of, I mean us prisoners, who was known as the scum of the earth. Which was not too far off the mark.

Governor Dawes said, The chaplain tells me you like to read, Bobby. Is that right? I said it was right and that I enjoyed reading very much. He looked at the guard standing next to me holding the cuffs and said, Well, Toby, old Henry's gone, so maybe this young feller would like to take over the Stuart library. The guard give me a sideways look and said, Maybe, but he did not sound convinced.

The governor looked back at me and said, How about it, Bobby? I thanked him for the offer and said I would do my best. He will do his best, Dawes said to the guard. See that he does. And that is how I come to be looking after the library all them years. I was moved to a cell on the upper floor of C Wing, above the library.

Reading saved my life in that place in them early years when I was still innocent of the ways of some men. So I always reckoned it was Irie saved my life from teaching me to read in the first place. I read every one of them seven hundred books they had in Stuart twice each. And I wrote letters for prisoners who could not write. I read to friends in prison who liked to hear the stories but could not read themselves, and I taught a few to read too. One of their favourite books was *Man-Shy*, the story of a heifer. I do not know why but the men, some of them vengeful and hard in their minds, loved to hear this story, and were like children with it, demanding to have it read to them over and over. It was written by a writer called Frank Dalby Davison, and no one has heard of him now. I would see a smile creep into the eyes of men I thought lost to all decency when the red heifer makes her bid for freedom.

It was in Stuart Prison that I become a reader and a writer. I was always building on the knowledge given me by Irie Collins. There was quiet hours in the library and it was not long before I began to write letters to Irie. I did not have no address for her so I just kept the letters in a box, each with its date on it. In the letters I went over everything that happened to us and I tried to get the truth of it clear and back into some order so she would understand that I had never betrayed her trust. Even though I knew she was never going to see those letters I got a satisfaction from writing them and they helped me to understand things myself. Sitting there in the quiet hours of the library writing to her I always felt me and Irie was talking to each other. It was a precious time for me.

I was twelve years in Stuart when I got the letter from Irie. I had never had no visitor after Charley and I had never had no letter till Irie's letter come that day. When I went in to open up the library in the morning I seen the letter lying on the desk where the guard must have put it for me to find. I read my name on the front of the envelope and I picked it up and held it. It had been opened and passed for me to read by the authorities and there was the blue prison stamp on each page of it. I knew in my guts who it was from. I sat down and unfolded the blue sheets of paper and read the whole letter over three or four times. I kept it and have copied it in here word for word. This is Irie's letter after twelve years of silence from her. It was on blue paper with no lines, which made me feel it was even more special than if it had been on plain white lined paper like they give us in the gaol.

Dear Bobby,

You will be surprised to get this letter from me. I know that. But I don't know if you will be pleased. I imagine you have forgotten me long ago and said in your mind good riddance to that girl. I have never forgotten you and our short time together at Mount Hay before the tragedy of that day at Coal Creek. I hardly dare mention Coal Creek to you, but if I am to write to you at all I must be honest and give you my reasons for getting in touch after such a long silence. You might have expected to hear from me and to have received my support at the time of your trial twelve years ago, but I was not able to give you my support as I was a minor and in a strange way I did not want to give it. You will not understand this, and I did not understand it myself, but I just wanted to be as far away in my mind from what happened as I could get. Seeing Miriam lying there dead has never left me. My little sister was alive one minute and sleeping in the cot with her arm over me and she was dead the next. I could not accept it. Some part of me still does not accept it and never will so long as I live. I will not lie to you about any of that now. It has not been easy for me to write and I have many fears about doing it. My biggest fear is that you and Ben Tobin blamed me for what happened that day and that you have never forgiven me and you may even hate the memory of me.

My mother put me into a boarding school in Brisbane and for six years I lived there more or less happily and as if I was

281

a different person from the girl you knew in the ranges. Mum continued to live in Townsville but I did not always come home for the holidays. Except for Christmas I usually stayed with a friend in Brisbane or on the Gold Coast. But Coal Creek and Mount Hay stayed with me like a private shadow. I lived in those early days after Mount Hay in a strangely private world of guilt and remorse for the stupidity of my actions and never for one day ceased to go over and over in my mind how differently things would have worked out if I had not been so stubborn and insisted on running away. It was the stupidest action of my life. I blamed myself for everything that happened—for my little sister's death and for the death of my father, and for Ben Tobin's death and for you being in gaol for the rest of your life. Ben and Deeds were kind to me and Miriam, and I repaid them with my silence.

The guilt of all this haunted me so much during my teenage years I always had this deep hidden place of worry going on that I could never admit to anyone. I find it difficult to write this to you even now, as it sounds as if I am complaining, while you have spent all these years without your freedom and you have far more reason than I do to complain of how unfair life has been to you. I will not go on and on about all that. It is too difficult and too painful and too complicated and too frightful to ever sort it all out or for me to ever feel completely free of it.

So why have I written to you now, you must be asking me? After I left school I did a shorthand and typing course and began working in the typing pool of a biscuit-making factory in Brisbane. I liked the work and the other girls and I met one of the junior accountants there and we got married. I was nineteen and he was twenty-three. We had a little girl. Allen changed towards me soon after we had Cynthia—that was not my choice of a name but was his mother's name and he insisted on it. He started staying out with his mates after work and drinking and my life became ugly and unpleasant. I don't wish to go into the details of all that but I left him just before Christmas last year and returned to Townsville with Cynth. My mother still lives in Townsville but we do not get on and except for Christmas and birthdays we don't see much of each other. I am working as a typist for a legal firm in Townsville and they are very nice people. I feel appreciated and respected at work and enjoy my time there.

Ever since I came back to Townsville I have thought every day of you being just up the road at Stuart. You are the only other person in the world who knows the real story of that day at Coal Creek and how it came about. I know I must speak with you if I am ever to get free of my guilt and the pressure of thinking of that day. Please forgive me for intruding into your life once again, Bobby, but I hope you will understand that I would love to somehow make amends for everything if I could possibly find a way.

If you do not hate the memory of me I should like to come and visit you. If I don't hear from you I will understand. Once again, please forgive me for pushing my way into your life again. You must wish you had never met me. There is only one thing I would like to ask of you. It is this: if you do hate me and do not wish to see me, I tell you now you must write the true story of Coal Creek or it will be lost forever and you and Ben will be thought of as nothing but cold-blooded killers, which you are not. I taught you to read and write all those years ago and if you do nothing else with that gift but write the true account of Coal Creek it will have been more than worthwhile. To see you redeem yourself would lift a load off my conscience that I cannot lift on my own. Forgive me for asking this of you. I have no claim over you.

She signed herself simply *Irie*.

I sat there at my desk in the quiet of the library, the sounds of the prison like the distant roar of water going down a chute, and I thought about that girl. I tried to see her in my mind but her likeness was gone and I had only my feeling of how much I had prized her friendship over the years and how it had helped me keep myself afloat in that place. There was hard things happened in Stuart but it is not my aim to speak of them here. I hated to think that Irie was burdened by feelings of guilt all these years for what happened and I wanted to call her up on the telephone right there and tell her it was none of it her fault. It took me a while to settle myself down enough to begin a letter back to her. When I was writing my letters to her all them years knowing she was never to read my words I wrote with ease and the words come to me without too much thinking about them. But now I could not think how to start and when I started I could not think how to go on. I started several times and screwed up each try and I got up and walked about the library and I looked out into the corridor and seen men coming and going, then I went back and I sat down again and I wrote to her that I would like to see her if she wished to pay me a visit.

I do not have the letter I sent her, but I remember telling her that I did not see how she was to blame for nothing that happened that morning out at Coal Creek, but that it was something like a sudden accident that no one seen coming and we was all taken by surprise. I said I had not expected her to ever wish to speak to me again and was very glad she had written to me. I do not know if I told her the whole truth of how I felt about her getting back in touch because I did not want to scare her away. Seeing her handwriting and reading her words of sorrow and suffering I was filled with a powerful emotion for her, which I knew must have scared her if I had told her of it.

The morning she come to the prison I was very nervous to see her. You will not believe me, but it is true all the same that

I was more nervous of seeing Irie than I had been of facing the hangman. Life plays such tricks on us.

She was sitting waiting for me when I come into the visitors' square. I recognised her at once. She was no longer the girl of twelve I had known but was grown into a smart young woman in her middle twenties. There was no mistaking her. She stood up when she seen me coming and we faced each other across the desk. The guard told us to sit down and we sat down. We said stupid things like, How are you? about ten times and give replies like, I'm real good. Then suddenly we both laughed and that was it, we was ourselves again with each other. She started to cry and I felt like crying myself and I was not allowed to reach across and touch her and that was the hardest thing for me. She apologised for crying and we laughed some more. She got her hankie out of her handbag and wiped her eyes and said she must look a mess. I had never seen no woman more beautiful but I did not have the courage to say so.

I decided then that I would give her all them letters I had written to her. I asked her if she had ever been back to Mount Hay. She had not been back and did not know what had happened to Deeds and Ben's child. Irie was working as a typist in a lawyer's office and she said she would make some enquiries and find out. We talked a while about Deeds and of her and Ben's baby, which was a way of not talking about ourselves. She said them two was the hidden victims of Coal Creek. I asked Irie where her own kid was and she said she was at kinder. She was four years of age and was very bright, Irie said. She was proud of her, I could see that. You will meet her, she said. I'll bring her with me next time I come in to see you. We did not talk about the things in her letter or her guilt or my own feelings. That was all too big and we was pressed for time. We was both emotional, I believe, at finding we was still Irie and Bobby together. It was the greatest feeling I ever had in my life and it made me wonder if I had ever understood anything at all or was just skimming over the top of life.

We did not say nothing about it, but when we laughed together was when we knew we was close and always had been. There was no covering that. When our time was up she said, I will come next week. I said I would wait for her. That was when I seen the tears in her eyes again, just as she was turning away. I watched till she was gone and seen her look back from out beyond where the guard stood.

. . .

Irie come to see me every week for two years until I got my parole and I told her I had started writing this account and that pleased her. The authorities would not allow me to pass over to her my bundle of letters, in which she would have seen the strength she had been for me. They wanted to read them all first and I would not permit that to happen. So them letters stayed with me till I got out. Irie only missed coming to see me once, and that was when her daughter was sick with a bad cold.

I wanted to help her come to the knowledge that there was no blame for her to take, and that we was all part of what happened, and it was just a real bad mistake. She told me she only had her mother's account of things to go on and needed to talk to me about the details. You are the only other person in the world who knows the truth of it. She said when she woke at the sound of the shotgun and come out the side door of Ben's place, Deeds holding her back, she seen her mother on her knees and thought she had been shot. Everyone seemed to be shooting at each other, she said. All I could think of was to get to my mother's side. She did not get on well with her mother, she said. Mum and me always had a bit of a problem. Miriam was Mum's shining star of hope and when she lost Miriam she lost her joy in living and never recovered it. Irie told me, Mum is bitter and is closed off from her despair. She blames me and she blames you and she blames herself for encouraging you with your reading. Irie said, I have tried to remind her that encouraging you the way she did when you first came into our home was a good and generous thing for her to do and was not the cause of the tragedy but only part of our lives as they was then. But Mum can't talk about it without getting upset. I go to see her whenever I can bear it, but neither of us enjoys my visits.

Irie found out my mare Mother died of snake bite in the paddock behind the pub where Chiller had kept her. When she told me this news I just said I had expected to hear something of that kind. The saddest things Irie found out through her enquiries was that the government men come out to Mount Hay and took Deeds and Ben's child away from her and that Deeds did not know where the kid was taken to and the government men would not tell her. Irie was going on with her enquiries to try and find the boy. Deeds had lived with Rosie for some years until Rosie passed away. I never said nothing to Irie about it, but in my heart I knew Rosie had put one of them Old Murri curses on Ben for beating her boy Orlando and that curse had stayed on him and bitten into his life and had brought on the conditions for his destruction. I never even told myself this in so many words, but I knew it. I knew it the way my mother knew such things. It was there, like a buried death you cannot speak of.

. . .

My parole come through after I had been inside for fourteen years. Governor Dawes asked me to come and see him. This time he stood up and come around his desk and shook my hand and he looked into my eyes and smiled and he wished me luck. You did well, Bobby, he said. He told me he was leaving Stuart himself and a new reforming governor from Ireland was coming to take on the job. When he told me the government was talking seriously now of doing away with the death penalty we looked on each other as equals, two men. And that was it. I shook Dawes' hand and wished him luck with his new job. He was always glad to know a prisoner who did not end up hating him, like most of them did.

Me and Irie was never allowed to touch each other during them two years of her visits to the prison. We never said the word love but it was there between us from that first day when we laughed and cried together at the same time. We knew then we had always been meant for each other, but we did not dare say so. We both dreamed of being able to reach out and touch each other. But we kept it as a dream. It was too powerful a feeling to ever talk about so long as I was not free. If we had let it out into the open it would have destroyed us with the ache of it. So we never said nothing about it. But it was in our hearts and in our eyes every time we seen each other. Them last two years took longer to pass for me than the first twelve years. I was afraid I would die or be killed before I had the chance to get paroled and to see Irie on the outside in the real world where we could have our freedom. I daydreamed all the time about this and my fear of not ever having it was so big it made me ill.

. . .

They give me my clothes back and the morning I stepped out of Stuart I was wearing my old hat again and knew myself a free man. I seen Irie waiting for me in the road with her little girl beside her. She come up to me and I do not think we could speak. She reached and took my hand and held it in her own hand and we walked down that road away from the prison hand in hand. It was like she had claimed me. By then we both knew we was going back to Mount Hay, where we belonged. We was going to try our luck out there together. Later I give her my bundle of old letters and this account. Together they was my understanding of the events that was locked in both our souls for the rest of our lives. Just like we was locked to each other. The grip of Irie's fingers in mine as we walked down the open road that morning was more than I can speak of.

ACKNOWLEDGEMENTS

I would like to express my heartfelt thanks to my publisher, Annette Barlow, to my UK publisher Clare Drysdale, to Siobhán Cantrill, to Wenona Byrne and to Ali Lavau and the team at Allen & Unwin. My thanks are due also to the poet Ross Donlon, who first dragged this story out of me.